THE SHERLOCK FILES

CASES: UNSOLVED

BOOK 2

THE
BEAST OF BLACKSLOPE

TRACY BARRETT

SQUARE
FISH

HENRY HOLT AND COMPANY
NEW YORK

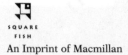

SQUARE
FISH

An Imprint of Macmillan

THE BEAST OF BLACKSLOPE. Copyright © 2009 by Parachute Publishing, LLC. All rights reserved. Printed in the United States of America by R. R. Donnelley & Sons Company, Harrisonburg, Virginia. For information, address Square Fish, 175 Fifth Avenue, New York, NY 10010.

Square Fish and the Square Fish logo are trademarks of Macmillan and are used by Henry Holt and Company under license from Macmillan.

Library of Congress Cataloging-in-Publication Data
Barrett, Tracy.
The Beast of Blackslope / by Tracy Barrett.
p.   cm. — (Sherlock files ; 2)
Summary: Xena and Xander Holmes, an American brother and sister spending a year in England, use clues in their ancestor Sherlock Holmes's casebook as they try to solve the mystery of a monster threatening a peaceful country village where a documentary film is being made.
ISBN 978-0-312-65918-9
[1. Brothers and sisters—Fiction. 2. Documentary films—Production and direction—Fiction. 3. England—Fiction. 4. Mystery and detective stories.] I. Title.
PZ7.B275355Be 2009   [Fic]—dc22   2008036941

Originally published in the United States by Henry Holt and Company
First Square Fish Edition: March 2011
Square Fish logo designed by Filomena Tuosto
Book designed by Greg Wozney
www.squarefishbooks.com

10 9 8 7 6 5 4

AR: 4.2 / LEXILE: 630L

BOOK 2 THE SHERLOCK FILES

THE

BEAST OF BLACKSLOPE

CHAPTER 1

Owoo-oo-ooo! The sound drifted through the air to the park where Xena and Xander Holmes were lying on their stomachs in the grass.

"What was *that*?" Xena sat up and pushed back her long dark hair. The eerie wailing sound had come from way off in the distance. It interrupted the Game she and Xander were playing and made her skin prickle.

Xander stared toward the woods. "Um, a siren?" He didn't really believe it though. That had been a *weird* noise. It gave him goose bumps.

"I guess." Xena wasn't convinced either. "A wolf, maybe? Do they have wolves here in England?" She knew Xander had been reading up on natural history for school. Xander had a photographic memory. He would remember any mention of wolves—especially because he had a phobia about wild animals.

"Nope." Xander shook his head. "No wild ones, anyway. The English killed them all by the eighteenth century. And there can't be a wolf sanctuary or anything like that near here or Mom and Dad would have definitely mentioned it. And I would have convinced them to pick someplace else for vacation."

"Well, maybe a dog, then." But Xena still felt uncomfortable. She'd never heard a dog make such a spooky sound. And now she felt that there was something creepy about the quiet town square in this little village. She shivered and decided to change the subject. If Xander thought there were wolves, or even something like them, nearby, he'd refuse to do any of the outdoor activities their parents had planned. "Let's play some more," Xena said. "It's still two-one, your favor."

Their father had taught them the Game, and his father had taught him, and his father had taught *him*, all the way back to the inventor of the Game: their great-great-great-grandfather Sherlock Holmes. They had found out only a few weeks ago that they were descended from the famous detective, and they had already solved one of the cases in his notebook of unsolved mysteries.

The Game was a good way to sharpen their detecting skills. The rules were simple: figure out something about passersby—like their job, where they come from, or what kind of mood they're in—just by observing them.

"I wonder where everyone went," Xander said. "It's not dark yet, and there were lots of people around until a few minutes ago. How can we play the Game?"

"Here comes somebody." Xena narrowed her eyes at the figure walking down the side of the road next to the park. Xander was getting too good at the Game, maybe even better than she had been at his age. But she was two years older, and she was determined to win this round.

"Hmmm," Xander muttered. It was a kid about twelve years old, like Xena. How can I figure him out? he wondered. There's nothing unusual about him.

The boy smiled as he passed. He had freckles, an upturned nose, and curly light brown hair. Xander saw a grin of triumph on Xena's face. Oh no—what had she seen?

"City kid!" she said, and Xander looked at the boy again. The boy stumbled over something and almost fell. He disappeared around a corner.

Xander groaned, because in that last second

he too had spotted the monthly Tube pass sticking out of the boy's back pocket. It looked just like the transit passes the two of them used to get to school and around London.

"Ha!" Xena said. "Two each! And the second one you got didn't really count."

"Did too," Xander said.

"Oh, okay." Xena could afford to be generous, because she had caught up. She stretched out on the grass and waited for another person to go by. This village seemed like a good place for their vacation, and she was excited about being somewhere other than London. Not that London wasn't a great city. She was really glad their dad had taken a one-year job there. She still missed her friends back home in the States, but she and Xander were attending a really cool school with kids from all over the world, and most of them were nice. She had even started liking Andrew Watson, whose great-great-great-grandfather had been Sherlock Holmes's best friend, and who went to their school.

Thinking of Sherlock reminded Xena of something. "Xander, you did remember to pack the notebook, didn't you?"

"Of course! You think I'd forget Sherlock's cold-case files? It's our best treasure."

A week after they had arrived in London, Xena and Xander found the secret meeting place for the Society for the Preservation of Famous Detectives—or the SPFD. The members of the SPFD believed that because Xena and Xander were descendants of Sherlock Holmes, they had the potential to be great detectives. The SPFD gave them Sherlock's notebook of unsolved cases, and Xander and Xena realized that some of those cases could still be cracked.

"We never would have found the lost painting without the clues in the notebook," Xena said. She and Xander had solved the case of a painting that had been missing for more than a hundred years.

"It would be so cool to solve another mystery," Xander said. "Not much chance of that on vacation though. Do you think—"

Ooo-ooo-OOOOOOO! They both froze as the howl drifted down from the forest. It started long and low, rose to a higher pitch, then dropped again before dying out.

"No *way* that was a siren!" Xena said. "Let's find out what it was!" She leaped up and ran in the direction of the eerie sound. When Xander didn't answer she glanced over her shoulder.

Xander had disappeared.

CHAPTER 2

Xander!" Xena called. Where had he gone? Had something sneaked up behind them and—

Oh, there he was, going into the bed-and-breakfast. Their father was standing at the door. "Didn't you hear me calling you?"

"Sorry," Xena said as she reluctantly headed into the B and B. "I was listening to something else." The truth was, she was still thinking about it. She'd never heard anything like that howl. She wished she could investigate it right now, because she knew that whatever made it might not stick around.

"Well, what do you think of our home away from home?" their dad asked.

When they first arrived in town, she and Xander had dumped their bags inside the door of the B and B and then dashed out to the village square, relieved to be able to stretch their legs after the long car ride. Now Xena paused and took a good look at the place where they'd be staying for fall break.

"It's like a little cottage in a fairy tale!" she exclaimed, admiring the cozy room with its fireplace, soft-looking furniture, and flowered curtains. Xander was busy gathering up clothes that had spilled out of his backpack. He seemed to be avoiding her eyes.

"I'm so glad you like it, dear," said a woman in a flower-print dress. She had short, curly gray hair, and she looked tired. "My name is Mrs. Roberts. My husband and I own this B and B."

Xander looked around with interest. "Is this place really ancient?" He thought it was cool that so many of the houses in England were so much older than the ones in their neighborhood back in Florida.

"It was built in the early seventeen hundreds," Mrs. Roberts told him. "We're so fond of the house's long history. It was used as quarters for visitors' servants when the family still lived in the Chimington Arms, before they moved to the manor."

"Oh, the Chimington Arms. Is that the hotel down the road?" their mother asked.

"Yes." Mrs. Roberts set flowered plates around the table. "And the B and B next to us used to be the stable. It took our friends the Hendersons a long time to get the horse smell out of it, but it's a lovely place now. Still, I like ours the best. It's cozy, don't you think?"

"It certainly is," their father said. "And it's nice of you to make us supper. B and B stands for 'bed and breakfast,' not 'bed and breakfast and supper.' We weren't expecting such a delicious meal this late in the day."

"Oh, it's just some sandwiches." Mrs. Roberts carried the empty tray out of the room, and Xena noticed that she was gripping it so tightly her knuckles were white. It can't be that heavy, Xena thought. She looks worried.

"When Mrs. Roberts comes back, let's ask her if she knows what that noise was," Xander whispered to Xena. She nodded and gave him a thumbs-up sign.

As they ate, the members of the Holmes family looked over the brochures that were heaped all around.

"Tour the Picturesque Downs on Horse-back," Xena read aloud. "What are downs?"

"They're round hills covered with grass," Xander answered. Xena sighed. Sometimes it was hard having a younger brother who was such a know-it-all.

Their father picked up another pamphlet. "Anyone interested in Wild Herb Walks?"

"No," Xena and Xander answered together.

Xena found a pad of paper and drew lines down it in three columns, headed MUST DO, MAYBE, and NO WAY.

"Here's information about the sale, Mom," Xander said. He handed her a photocopied sheet of paper.

"Thanks, hon," she said. "I can't wait to see all those wonderful antiques in that old house! Xena, put that in the must-do column, okay?"

"Why are they selling antiques in a house?" Xander asked. "Don't they sell them in a store?"

"The family's moving," his mother explained. "They're selling a lot of their old things. The house is for sale too."

Mrs. Roberts came back in. "Let me show you around quickly before you go to bed," she said, smoothing her apron nervously. Xander opened his mouth as though to ask her about the howl, but Xena shot him a look that made him close it again. "Don't interrupt her," she whispered. Xena was good at picking up on unspoken thoughts. She sensed Mrs. Roberts was upset about something, and she was hoping that if they just listened, they'd find out what it was.

"This is the breakfast room," Mrs. Roberts told them. It had yellow curtains and a rag rug and a round table with enough spaces for eight around it. "Please feel free to make yourselves snacks whenever you like. Just leave the dirty crockery in the sink. Over here"—she gestured to her right—"is the sitting room. I think you Americans call it the living room?" Their mom nodded as they all got up and followed Mrs. Roberts into the warm-looking room with a fireplace and a braided rug. "There's a telly," she went on, "but we don't get many stations, I'm afraid."

"What about a computer?" Xena asked.

"I'm afraid we just have an old one for keeping the accounts."

"No Internet?" Xena was disappointed when Mrs. Roberts shook her head. How was she supposed to keep in touch with her friends?

"Cheer up," her father said. "We'll keep you so busy exploring ancient ruins and taking hikes that you won't even miss them."

"Who's that?" Xander was looking at one of the old-fashioned photos on the mantelpiece. Mrs. Roberts didn't answer. Curious, Xena glanced at her. Was it her imagination, or had the woman turned pale?

"It's—she was my great-great-grandmother," Mrs. Roberts finally said.

Xander continued examining the picture. "She looks sad."

There was another awkward silence, and then Mrs. Roberts rubbed her eyes. "I'm off to bed," she said. "Sleep well, and I'll see you in the morning."

"Boy, she goes to bed early," Xander said after she had left.

"What's the name of this town again, Mom?" Xena asked, looking at a map in a guidebook.

"Blackslope," Mrs. Holmes replied, and added as she left the room with their father, "Don't stay up too late."

Xena turned back to the map but Xander nudged her. "Blackslope!" he said, his voice high with excitement. "Sherlock's been here!"

CHAPTER 3

U h-uh," Xena said.

"Yeah-*huh*," Xander said. "Come on, I'll show you! Sherlock *has* been here!"

They raced each other up the stairs. As usual, long-legged Xena won.

"Which room is mine?" Xander called.

"The one on the left," their father called back.

It was a neat room, with old paintings on the walls and a skylight over the bed. Xander opened his suitcase and rummaged through his things, tossing out socks, a book, and his MP3 player. Finally he pulled out the cold-case notebook that had belonged to their great detective ancestor Sherlock Holmes. He leafed through it quickly, his eyes flickering over the pages. *Aha!*

"See?" He pointed at a page in triumph.

Xena sat down next to him. "'The Beast of Blackslope,'" she read, and then looked at Xander. "A beast!"

"Right," he said, rapidly scanning the page. He tried not to let Xena see how uncomfortable the idea of a beast made him. He hoped his hands wouldn't leave sweat marks on the old paper. "Sherlock was called to Blackslope Manor to investigate some mysterious beast. And no one ever figured out what kind of animal it was."

"Cool!" Xena said. "Maybe it's still here, howling. It's got to be the same Blackslope, right?"

Xander nodded. "See, Sherlock talks about someone named Lord Chimington, who asked him to investigate. When Mrs. Roberts said Chimington, the name rang a bell." Xena groaned at the pun.

Xander grinned at her. He was feeling better. He reminded himself that any beast that had been around a century ago would surely be dead by now—if it ever even existed. He went on, "But I couldn't remember where I'd heard it. Then when Mom said Blackslope, I knew I hadn't heard it, I'd *read* it right here!"

"Let me see," Xena said, and her brother slid the notebook over so that half of it was on her lap. The page was dated 24 August in their ancestor's now-familiar handwriting. Beneath the date, notes were scrawled. One item read, "Large shape at cook's bedroom window after midnight—long hairs found snagged on sill next morning."

Xena bent more closely over the book. "What's that?" She pointed at a sketch of a strange creature.

"Hmmm." Xander took back the casebook and examined the sketch. "It looks like a gorilla, kind of. But also like a Sasquatch or something. Check out those fangs. Creepy." He shivered.

"And look at this footprint!" Xena pointed at an outline. Some numbers were scribbled next to it. "Are those measurements? That thing must have been huge!"

"Wow, a mysterious beast! And it howled at night." Their eyes met. "You don't think . . ." Xander's voice trailed off. He swallowed. It was hard to imagine something so ferocious-looking in this gentle landscape, but their great ancestor had clearly come here looking for just that beast. "Didn't Sherlock once solve a case like this in Dartmoor?"

Xena nodded. "The case about the Hound of the Baskervilles. It was one of his most famous cases ever. That's probably why he was called in on this one."

"Sherlock said this beast howled at dusk. That's sunset."

24 August

Noises at night – something large moving in woods

The Beast of Blackslope

Asked by Lord Chimington to investigate

Chickens, sheep attacked

Abominable Snowman?

18"

6"

Large shape at cook's bedroom window after midnight – long hairs found snagged on sill next morning.

Howling at dusk

Unsolved

Dogs barked frantically

SHERLOCK • HOLMES
221B BAKER STREET LONDON

"No," Xena said. "I mean, duh, yes, dusk means sunset, but no, it couldn't be the same beast. Sherlock was here more than a hundred years ago. No animal could live that long."

"Tortoises and parrots do. And what about the Loch Ness monster? People have been saying they've seen that for a long time."

Xena was unconvinced. "Well, maybe some kind of reptile or bird could live that long, but not a mammal."

"Oh, quit being so negative. It could be that this beast is the offspring of the original one. Or maybe there's a whole herd of them! This is a pretty remote area. It's possible that some creature could hide in the woods for a long time. Maybe it's been living off chickens and squirrels and things for the last century." The idea was creepy but cool.

Xander fell silent. On the one hand, he couldn't wait to take on another case. He and Xena had discovered that they loved detecting. It must be in their blood. But a beast? He looked at the picture again. Could something like that ever have existed? And if it had, what did it do with those claws? He shivered and the book started sliding off his lap.

Xena grabbed it. "Careful!" she warned. "If we figure out what was howling last night and it turns out to be Sherlock's beast, we could close another one of his cold cases. That would be awesome! Let's see if he left any other notes that can help."

They examined the page for more clues.

"That's strange," Xena finally muttered. "That footprint looks like one a flat-footed person would make. See? There's no arch. And look—it has only four toes. Weird! Don't mammals have five toes?"

"Yes, but sometimes one is on their wrist or ankle or whatever it is and only four show up in the print. That's mostly big cats, though, like lions, and this beast doesn't sound like a lion."

"It doesn't sound like *anything* normal," Xena said.

Xander turned the page, reading over the notes. Sherlock's final scribble on the page read: "Unsolved."

"Okay," Xena said. "I say let's go exploring first thing tomorrow and see what we can find out."

"I'll get to work in the library," Xander offered. "I can speed-read through old newspapers and learn everything there is to know about the beast in record time."

"I'll go with you." Xena knew her brother wasn't boasting about the speed-reading but just stating a fact. It really would be useful if he could find out more than the little bit Sherlock Holmes had written.

Xena went to her room, leaving Xander in his. Suddenly he noticed that the room's single lightbulb was dim and cast creepy shadows. He hurriedly dug out a nightshirt and his toothbrush. He almost wished he was sharing a room with Xena. It was so quiet and so dark out here in the country, and his parents' room was on the other side of the house.

He put on his headphones and listened to some music on the new MP3 player. Their mother's job as a product tester for an electronics company came in handy sometimes. He and Xena got to try out all the latest gadgets, and he especially liked this one.

Usually the music would help him sleep, but tonight he felt wide awake, even though he was in the kind of bed he'd always wanted. It had a puffy coverlet that settled around him like a cocoon. When he finally did go to sleep, he had strange dreams about beasts. Something huge and shaggy stretched its four-clawed paws at him and bared yellow teeth in a long, mournful howl.

Xander popped up, his heart pounding. For a moment, he couldn't tell if the howl had been part of a dream or was real. He got up and looked out the window. Then the sound started again. Thinking fast, he hit the Record key on his MP3 player. Almost immediately the sound died away. Had he managed to record any of it? The thought of hearing that sound again all alone in the dead of night made him shiver. Better to listen after the sun came up.

It was really dark here, far away from the streetlights and office lights that stayed on all night in London. The tiny sliver of moon that shone through the branches of the enormous tree in the garden didn't help much. He strained his eyes but couldn't see a thing. And there was no way he was going outside by himself in the dark when something out there was making that weird noise.

He went back to bed and although he managed to fall asleep, he had unsettling dreams about beasts for the rest of the night.

When he went down to breakfast the next morning, Xena was already eating her favorite English breakfast: crumpets. There were three kinds of jam, homemade, his mother said, and hot chocolate as well as tall glasses of juice.

"Wow!" Xander said.

"Better hurry or Xena will eat all those

crumpets," their father teased. Xena said something but he couldn't understand it around her big mouthful.

"Plenty more where they came from." It was Mrs. Roberts, and if anything, she appeared even more tired and tense than she had the night before. She was carrying a tray with two cups of coffee on it. She put them in front of the adults and started clearing away dirty dishes.

As Xander smeared a crumpet with red jam he asked, "Did anyone hear an animal howl last night?"

"Nope," his father said. "You must have been dreaming."

"No way," Xander protested. "I recorded it! Listen." He pulled out his MP3 and punched the Play key, hoping that something had made it onto the recording.

It had. The last few seconds of that unearthly wail filled the room.

Xena swallowed a gigantic mouthful. "I bet it was that beast!" she managed to say. But before Xander could answer, they heard a soft moan. Mrs. Roberts was swaying and her face had turned ashy pale. Mrs. Holmes leaped to her feet but before she could reach her, Mrs. Roberts dropped the tray.

CHAPTER 4

Mrs. Holmes caught Mrs. Roberts. "Are you okay?" she asked.

"Lina!" A thin man with white hair hurried in. "My dear! What happened?"

Mrs. Roberts passed the back of her hand shakily across her forehead. "I—I don't know, Nigel. I suddenly felt giddy."

"Here, let me take you up to bed." The man half turned to the Holmes family and said, "Shan't be a minute." As he and Mrs. Roberts left the room he said, "Now, dear, you're not worried about that again, are you?"

Xena and Xander looked at each other. Worried about *what* again? They knelt down next to the mess, carefully picking up broken dishes and dabbing at the drops of coffee and smears of jam with a paper napkin.

When the man returned, Mrs. Holmes asked, "How's Mrs. Roberts?"

"Oh, fine, fine," he said hurriedly. "No need to worry. She hasn't been sleeping well lately. A nap will fix her right up."

His words sound more cheerful than his voice, Xena thought.

Mr. Holmes stood. "Well, we'll be getting out from underfoot soon. Please let us know if there's anything we can do." He and Mrs. Holmes went to the sitting room, and Xena and Xander set out to find the local library.

It was a beautiful day—cool, but with that edge of warmth that means the afternoon will be just right. A little breeze ruffled the grass in the park where they had been playing the Game the evening before, and a bird was singing so loudly in a tree above them it almost hurt Xena's ears.

They turned onto the sidewalk and saw a blond-haired young woman coming out of the shed between their B and B and the one next door. She looked to be about the same age as their cousin Kelly, who had left for college the past fall. She carried a large black case that pulled her over to the side with its weight. She was chatting with another young woman, who was shorter and had dark wavy hair. The blond one caught sight of Xena and Xander and nudged her companion, who turned to look at them.

"Come on, Emma," the dark-haired one said. "We've heaps to do today."

Xena automatically scanned her for a clue. Pink top, regular jeans, white running shoes. The blonde paused and swiped the hair off her face with the back of her hand, and then switched her grip on the case.

Xander focused on the case. What could be in it? It had hard sides, like an old-fashioned suitcase, but it was the wrong shape. It was almost exactly a cube. Black, with metal caps reinforcing its corners. She's got to be strong, he thought. I wonder if that's a clue. Maybe she's a bodybuilder—or a gymnast.

Xena was thinking, Could that be a musical instrument? They're sometimes in big black cases like that. But she couldn't think of an instrument with that shape.

Each knew that the other was silently playing the Game. They looked at each other with raised eyebrows, their signal for "Give up?"

Xander nodded and broke into a trot to catch up with the older girls. He flashed his most winning smile, the one that made his dimples stand out, and cocked his head appealingly. The young women slowed down and smiled back at him. They chatted for a minute, and then gave

Xander a friendly wave as he went back to where Xena was waiting.

"The blond one is Emma and the dark-haired one is Katy," he reported. "They're university students from London and they're here on fall break, like us."

"What was in that case?"

Xander shrugged. "I asked them but they didn't say. Nothing special, I guess."

"I don't think it was clothes. It looked too heavy. And what a weird shape! It would be hard to fit into a car, and it's so square it kept banging into Emma's legs as she walked. I bet they're hiding something."

"Oh, come on," Xander scoffed. "There isn't a mystery *everyplace*."

It was Xena's turn to shrug. Maybe Xander was right, but such an odd container must hold something important or Emma wouldn't be straining so hard to carry it—where?

"Should we follow them?" Xena asked.

"I think we should go to the library like we planned," Xander said. "We need more information on Sherlock's unsolved case."

They asked a woman for directions and soon found themselves at a small building with a sign saying BLACKSLOPE LENDING LIBRARY in front of it.

The door was ajar, and as they wiped their feet on the mat, raised voices came from inside.

"It's back, I tell you!" a man was saying. "Or maybe it never left!"

What was back? And why did the man sound so upset? Xander moved away from the door to allow Xena to poke her head in, not risking even a whisper for fear that the people inside would notice him.

Somehow Xena had always been able to blend in with her surroundings. Her mother called this trick "Xena's cloak of invisibility," and it was a useful skill in a lot of situations, especially when Xena wanted to listen in on a conversation.

The room was filled with bookshelves made of dark wood. A desk with a green-shaded lamp had a sign saying HEAD LIBRARIAN. Xena managed to maneuver herself closer and heard a woman's voice say, "What nonsense! How could that be?"

"I don't know," the man replied. "But it's acting just like the old stories say, howling at sundown and crashing through fences. Old Fred found this hanging off the splinters of a broken fencepost. We're not safe in our beds, especially those of us who live south of town, like me. That's where the disturbance is coming from."

Xena crept in. She could see the man,

who was stocky and middle-aged, showing the librarian a tuft of what looked like stained wool.

The man went on, "And my missing sheep hasn't reappeared."

"Oh, surely it just went wandering through a gap in your fence or—" the librarian began to protest, but the man kept talking.

"I know where to look, though—south of my farm, toward the manor. History is repeating itself, I tell you. It's the *beast*!"

At the word "beast" Xander gave an involuntary start and brushed against the bell dangling from the door. It clanged loudly and the two adults stopped talking. The man pushed past them and hurried out the door.

Xena rolled her eyes at Xander. He shrugged to say sorry, then walked inside.

The lady behind the desk was a slender woman with short light brown hair. "Now then," she said to them briskly. "How may I help?"

"We're looking for local newspapers," Xander said.

"There's today's edition of the *Blackslope Gazette*," the librarian said, pointing at a pile of papers on a round table. "And the editions for the past week are shelved behind it."

"No, sorry," Xena said hastily. "We mean old

ones. From, um, maybe a hundred years ago?"

The librarian looked at her sharply, as if she was going to ask a question but didn't. Xena and Xander had noticed that English people tried harder than most Americans not to appear nosy, and this time they were glad of it.

"We're here on vacation," Xander explained. "We're interested in local history. We thought it would be fun to get background on some of the places we're going to visit." He smiled up at her and her face softened.

"Well, how lovely, dear!" She came out from behind her desk and headed toward the shelves behind the table. "Most children your age wouldn't be—" She stopped. "Well, I wonder—" She stopped again.

"What is it?" Xena came up behind her.

The librarian was staring at a bare spot in the middle of stacks of yellowing newspapers. "It's most peculiar." The librarian put her hand in the empty area as though she couldn't believe there was nothing there. "I know this case was full of copies of the *Blackslope Gazette* just last week. That's when I straightened the shelves. I would have noticed if any were missing. And now a whole stack is gone!"

"Gone?" Xena asked. "You mean, stolen?"

The librarian didn't answer. "Maybe someone just checked them out," Xena said.

The librarian shook her head. "They're old and fragile. We don't allow them to circulate."

It seemed rude to ask for the librarian's help when she was obviously upset, but they still wanted to do their research.

"Which ones are missing?" Xena asked. The librarian looked at the tag on the shelf. She seemed too stunned to speak, so Xena leaned over and looked for herself. Her heart sank. She silently pointed at the shelf tag, and Xander read it. The missing papers were from the last week of August, the same week Sherlock Holmes had come to investigate the sightings of the beast.

Xena pulled Xander aside while the librarian continued to stare at the shelf. "Do you know what this means?" Xena asked.

"There's a newspaper thief in Blackslope?"

"Quit kidding around!" She felt her heart thumping. "You know what I mean."

He nodded. "Someone else is interested in that same week. And it looks like they don't want anyone else to find out anything about it."

CHAPTER 5

Xander went back to where the librarian was still staring at the empty shelf and asked her, "Are there any copies of the newspapers? Or are they online someplace?"

The librarian pulled her hand off the shelf, straightened, and said sharply, "Online? Of course not. Paper has served humankind for thousands of years, and I see no reason to reduce something so noble to images on a screen. Online, indeed!"

"Can we look at some of the ones that are left?" Xander asked.

The librarian hesitated. "I don't know. Perhaps I should lock up the rest if they're going missing. They're irreplaceable."

"Please?" Xander asked. "We'll be very careful with them."

"Well, just for a few minutes. And stay where I can see you."

But after leafing through the papers that were before and after the missing ones, they found nothing helpful. The language was old-fashioned and sometimes hard to understand, and they couldn't find a single reference to a strange animal or unusual goings-on at night. Xena was ready to leave, but Xander was staring at an illustration on one of the inside pages.

"These pictures are amazing," he said. He pulled a tissue from his pocket and blew his nose. The papers were old and musty, making his nose run and his eyes itch.

Xena looked over his shoulder. He was bent over an engraving of a street scene in Blackslope with a caption reading *Lady Chimington's flower show attracts visitors from across the county*. Men with twirly mustaches and women in long dresses walked arm in arm down a street that was drawn with such detail that Xena and Xander recognized many of the shops they had seen that morning on their way to the library.

Yes, the illustrations were amazing, but this wasn't getting them any closer to solving the mystery. "Come on, Xander, let's go," Xena said, and they carefully returned the newspapers to their place and thanked the librarian.

"I wonder what's going on," Xena said as

they went down the stairs. "We thought we were just coming here for vacation, and now there are *three* mysteries: what the Beast of Blackslope was, and if it's back, and what happened to those newspapers."

"I don't know that missing hundred-year-old newspapers are really a mystery," Xander objected. "Anything could have happened to them. A cleaning person might have thought they were trash, or maybe someone borrowed them and forgot to check them out."

Xena shook her head. "No way. This town is full of secrets."

"Like what?"

"Well, for one thing, why did everyone disappear yesterday evening? One minute the streets were so full that we had our pick of subjects for the Game, and then—nobody. It wasn't really dark yet and the weather was nice, so where did they go all at once? And then there were those weird howls yesterday afternoon. And those girls wouldn't tell us what they were carrying. Those people in the library stopped talking when they saw us, and Mrs. Roberts is really jumpy. I bet she knows something."

"I wonder what made her drop the tray," Xander said.

Xena thought back. "It was right after I said that what you'd heard in the night must be the Beast. And just now the people in the library were talking about the Beast, and they sounded really upset about it. Maybe they all know something about this Beast, and they're keeping it a secret."

"Why would they do that? Why wouldn't they want people to know?"

"*I* don't know. That's what we'd have to investigate. Maybe somebody who lives here is up to something, and everyone wants to protect him because they don't want him to get into trouble."

"Or—" Xander hesitated. It sounded stupid.

"Or what?"

"Or what if it's some kind of demon? Or a curse on the town and they're ashamed?"

Xena didn't laugh. "I don't think that's it. I bet it's the same Beast from a hundred years ago. That means it's one of Sherlock's cases that's still open. We have a duty to solve it for him."

Xander nodded. Even though he wasn't too eager to investigate a savage-sounding creature, he felt the tie to their famous ancestor as strongly as his sister did. "Let's try to gather some clues and see what we can come up with."

"First," Xena said, "if people know something

and they're not talking, we have to try to listen in on some conversations."

"Your department."

Xena nodded. "And we have to find some way to go south of town and see if we can find the broken fence that guy was talking about. Those howls came from there." She pointed toward the forest. "That's south, right?"

"I think so," Xander said. It was broad daylight and from what they'd heard, the Beast prowled only at night. It would probably be okay if they went to check it out. Or at least that's what he told himself.

Xena and Xander had entered the main part of the village. The stores were small white buildings with wooden beams crisscrossing the walls—"half-timbered," their mother had called it—and identical reddish brown roofs. "They look like Snow White's cottage," Xena said.

"Yes, but where *is* everybody?" Xander wondered aloud. It seemed almost like a ghost town, and they were the only people on the sidewalk. Some of the stores were closed, which seemed odd in the middle of the week. CLOSED INDEFINITELY read a handwritten note on one door; FAMILY EMERGENCY read another. They passed a store with a sign saying ESTATE AGENT that displayed photographs of houses for sale in the window, with descriptions that made them all sound like palaces.

Xander stopped short. "Aha!"

"Aha what?"

"I know where we can do more research."

Xena looked around. "Where?"

"It's elementary, my dear Holmes." Xander grinned at her.

Xena rolled her eyes. "That line was old before you were born. What's elementary?"

In response, Xander pointed at a sign across the street. "'Tuttle's Antiquarian Books,'" he read. "If they have really old books, I bet we can do some research about the Beast!"

They crossed the street and went into the bookstore. It was empty except for a short, round man who sat in a wheelchair behind a small desk near the back. The nameplate on the desk read HAROLD TUTTLE. "Morning," he called. "What can I do for you?"

"We're looking for books on local history," Xena said.

"Right over here." The man rolled his chair past them and down a dark corridor.

Xander studied him as he passed. The man had thinning pale hair and wore black trousers and a black T-shirt. On the T-shirt were printed the words FRODO LIVES. On the legs of his trousers were several gray hairs.

"What's your cat's name, Mr. Tuttle?" Xander asked. "Gandalf, right?"

"That's ri—" The man broke off and stared at Xander. "Here, how'd you know my cat's name? How'd you even know I have a cat? And how'd you know *my* name?"

"I like finding things out about people, that's all. That line on your T-shirt is about *The Lord of the Rings*, and you have gray cat hairs on your pants. Gandalf the Grey is one of the main characters in *The Lord of the Rings*. So I figured you'd probably name your cat after him. And your name, well, it's on your nameplate."

"Just like Sherlock Holmes, you are," the man said.

Xander beamed. "He was our great-great-great-grandfather, actually!"

"Are you two detectives, then?"

"Well, sort of," Xena answered. "Xander and I are investigating one of Sherlock's old cases— the Beast of Blackslope. And I think you know all about it, Mr. Tuttle!"

CHAPTER 6

Now it was Xander's turn to be surprised. "No way!" he said. "How could you possibly figure that out, Zee?"

"Elementary, my dear Holmes," Xena said with a grin. "Mr. Tuttle wrote a book about the Beast." She pointed at the shelf where dozens of identical paperbacks leaned against each other forlornly. The spine on all of them read *The Beast: Blackslope's Monster*. Under it in larger letters was the name H. Tuttle.

"Good detective work!" Then the man's face fell. "My book is self-published, and it isn't selling too well. But the truth should be known, even if people round here want to pretend it never happened. They're afraid. Afraid to believe there might really be a Beast."

"So what do you think actually happened back then?" Xena asked.

"Well." Mr. Tuttle sat back and made a

steeple with his fingers. "Here's the real story. It's all in the book, of course, but I'll summarize for you.

"The last time the Beast appeared was in the early nineteen hundreds. The two people most involved were James and Adeline, the coachman and cook up at the manor. James was a great brute of a man—they say he could knock down a draft horse with one blow of his fist. And he had a jealous, evil temper, especially when it came to his wife.

"Adeline seemed quiet and meek, but James always swore that her mother had been a witch and that Adeline had learned spells and potions from her. If James ever raised a hand to her or their children, the next day he'd be clutching his stomach in agony, or all covered with spots, or shivering with a fever."

"You mean Adeline fed him poison!" Xena exclaimed.

Mr. Tuttle blinked at her. "No one ever caught her at it, but James said she did. Now I've lost my train of thought. Where was I? Oh, yes.

"Well, apparently one morning Adeline came to work in the great house, pale and trembling. She said James had put a curse on her. She didn't say what kind of curse, but she was clearly terrified. 'I am doomed,' she kept saying, and no one could tell her any different. And that very night the Beast made its first attack. A farmer near the manor found one of his sheep torn apart, as if by a ravenous monster."

"Ugh." Xander shuddered.

"The night after that, a young man coming home late from the pub was chased by a gigantic shaggy creature that he swore had foot-long claws and fangs. The next night, another farmer's chicken coop was destroyed and the chickens scattered. Each incident was nearer to the manor. Step-by-step, the Beast was making its way to its victim. And then it appeared out-side James and Adeline's window—they lived in a room built onto the back of the stables. Two days later . . ." Mr. Tuttle paused dramatically. "Adeline vanished. And she was never seen again."

"Sherlock's notes didn't say anything about a curse," Xena said.

Mr. Tuttle sniffed. "Perhaps the great detective wasn't as great as all that. Perhaps he didn't know about the curse. After all, he never solved the case."

Xena was stung at the insult to her ancestor. "Anyway, I thought Adeline was supposed to be the witch, not James. How would James know how to put a curse on her?"

Mr. Tuttle leaned forward. "Now that's an interesting question. Of course, there's no way to be sure. But I have a theory. There was a circus in town that summer. Circuses always have fortune-tellers and people like that. They camped on the grounds of the manor, in fact. I believe James found someone there to help him with the curse."

"Hmmm." Xena wasn't convinced.

"Scoff if you like," Mr. Tuttle said. "But if you're wise, you'll take care. Because the Beast is back!"

CHAPTER 7

Xander felt a sudden chill run up his spine even though he didn't *really* believe in monsters, and Xena couldn't hold back a gasp. Mr. Tuttle sounded so convincing.

"How do you know?" Xander asked uneasily.

"The signs are all around us. Surely you've heard the strange howls in the night. It's been going on for more than a week now. And something broke through a farmer's fence last night and took one of his sheep. All he found was some bloody wool. Exactly the way it happened more than a hundred years ago. History is repeating itself."

Xander's eyes widened. But before he could ask another question, the bell at the door tinkled, and Mr. Tuttle wheeled away to help the customer who had come in.

"What do you think?" Xander pitched his voice low so that Mr. Tuttle wouldn't hear.

"I don't believe it." Xena could be so very stubborn. "How do we know it isn't some vandal, like some kids who are bored out here in the country and wrecking things for the fun of it? Or some wild—"

She stopped herself but Xander knew she'd been about to say "wild animal."

He pretended not to notice. "Well, whatever it is, it's an awful lot like what Sherlock described."

"Exactly," Xena said. "Which means we should find out who—or what—is doing it and stop it if we can. That's what *he* would have wanted."

She didn't need to say whom she meant by "he," and Xander knew he couldn't argue. Being a descendant of the great Holmes was exceptionally cool, but having his book of unsolved cases was also a big responsibility.

Xena pulled a copy of Mr. Tuttle's book off the shelf and leafed through it. Xander looked over her shoulder.

"Who's that?" He pointed at a black-and-white photograph of a thin-faced woman in a dress with a high neck. Xena moved her thumb down from where it was covering the caption. "'Adeline Daniels,'" she read.

Xander looked up at Xena. "That's the cook!"

She could tell that something was bothering him. "What is it?"

"She looks familiar. I wonder—"

Just then the cell phone they shared rang. Xander fished it out and looked helplessly at it. It was one of their mom's new test products. It supposedly had great reception and could take excellent pictures and videos. The problem was that he hadn't figured out how to answer it.

"Give me that." Xena snatched the phone from him and punched a button. "Hello? Oh, hi, Mom. Okay, we'll be right there."

She punched another button and said to Xander, "We need to get back."

"Be careful!" Mr. Tuttle called after them. "The Beast is out there!"

"We will," Xena called back. "Thanks!"

"Do you think he could be right?" Xander asked his sister as they walked down the street. A chill went through him as he pictured the creature Mr. Tuttle had described. "Do you think the Beast really is some kind of demon? And now it's back?"

"Of course not. That's impossible."

Right, Xander told himself. Demons are impossible. But this time Xena's certainty didn't convince him. *Something* was out there making those awful howls. "Well then, how do you explain all the signs Mr. Tuttle talked about?"

Xena frowned. "I don't know. Yet."

Well then, how can you be so sure? Xander wanted to ask. But he didn't want Xena to know how much the idea of a demon beast spooked him. Instead he said, "Hey, look," and pointed to the window of the real estate office, which they were passing again. "Here's a sign for that sale Mom wants to go to. 'Antiques, heirlooms, one-of-a-kind family pieces,'" he read.

"Look, there are oil paintings too."

"And an 'eighteenth-century commode,'" Xander read. "Huh? They're selling an old *toilet*?"

A burst of laughter behind them made them turn around. A sandy-haired boy about Xander's age, wearing a soccer jersey, was standing on the sidewalk watching them. "A commode is like a bureau," he said. "You know, with lots of drawers to store things in?"

"Oh," Xander said. "Back home some people call a toilet a commode when they're trying to be polite."

"Back home is the States, right?"

Xena and Xander nodded.

"My name is Trevor," the boy went on. "And you're Xena and Xander."

"How did you know?" Xena asked.

"My grandparents own the B and B where you're staying," Trevor said. "I was spending the night at my friend's house when you got in, but my grandma told me about you this morning."

"You live with your grandparents?" Xander asked.

The boy nodded. "My parents travel a lot for business. They think it's important for me to have a stable environment so I stay with my grandparents. I like it here in Blackslope, but what I really want to do is go to Australia. Have you ever been?" They shook their heads. "I want to travel in the outback. I want to be a naturalist and study kangaroos and dingoes, and learn to play a didgeridoo."

"A what?" Xander's head was spinning from all the changes of subject.

"A didgeridoo," Trevor said. "It's a kind of Australian instrument. You blow into it. It looks sort of like a long wooden tube, and it sounds really cool."

"So if you want to be a naturalist, you must know a lot about the wildlife around here, right?" Xena asked.

"Sure." The boy shrugged. "Not that there's much. Rabbits, foxes—"

"What about the Beast of Blackslope?" Xena

asked. "Did you hear that howling last night?"

Trevor stopped talking as suddenly as if he had been a TV and someone had punched the Off button. For a second his mouth hung open, and then he shut it with a snap.

He cleared his throat. "What time did you hear a howl?"

"I don't know," Xena said. What an odd question. "We heard three, right, Xander?"

He nodded. "Two yesterday right at dusk and then I heard one in the middle of the night. It woke me up."

"I don't know what you heard," Trevor said. "But you'd better be careful."

"Careful about what?" Xander asked. But Trevor turned and walked rapidly away.

"I wonder why he doesn't want us looking for the Beast." Xena frowned.

"Maybe he's right," Xander said.

Xena knew she shouldn't but she couldn't help saying, "Xan, there's nothing dangerous out there. This is just a sleepy little—"

"How do *you* know?" he shot back. "Anyway, I'm not afraid!"

"You're not?"

"No way!" Just the idea of the Beast made him want to run all the way back to London. But he wasn't about to admit that to his obnoxious sister.

"Oh, come on." She sounded disgusted. "You've been afraid of wild animals ever since that raccoon bit you when you were little."

"Well, it was scary. And then I had to get all those shots. They really hurt. And anyway, *you're* afraid of being in small, tight places!"

"What does that have to do with anything? You're still afraid of wild animals, and we may be hunting for one."

"I've gotten over it." She rolled her eyes and this made him so furious that he spat out without thinking, "Fine. We'll go in the woods together to look for this Beast. And I bet I'll find it before you do!"

CHAPTER 8

There you are!" their father said when they pushed open the door of the B and B. "You're just in time. We need you to break a tie."

"A tie?" Xander asked. "About what?"

"Your mom wants to check out the preview at the sale."

"What's that?" Xena asked.

"They put everything that's going to be sold on display a day or two ahead," their mother explained. "That way you can examine it and have time to think about what you might want to buy and how much you want to spend."

Xena and Xander groaned. "And I want to take a hike," their father said. "I need to try out those new boots. So we thought we'd leave it up to you two."

"Hike!" they both said, and their mom laughed and said, "Okay, I know when I'm out-numbered. Which way should we go?"

Xander promptly said, "South." He glared at Xena, daring her to say something. He was going to prove to Xena that he wasn't afraid—and he was going to look for clues!

"Why south?" their father asked.

"That's the direction those woods are in, isn't it?" Xander asked. Their father nodded. "Well, don't you want to see some wildlife?"

"You? Wildlife?" Their mother looked surprised. "Anyway, I thought you liked London!"

"We do," Xena said. "We do, a lot. It's just that it will be nice to get out in the country."

"Okay," their mom said. "Let's get some picnic supplies so we can spend all day exploring."

"There's lots of cool stuff around the place we're going." Xena was reading the guidebook.

Xander was looking straight out the windshield—or the windscreen, as it was called here—and let her read to him. He knew if he read even a few words in a moving car, he'd get so carsick they'd have to pull over. "Like what?"

"Like the ruins of an old temple and rock formations and things."

Xander nodded, still looking ahead. A huge mass of something white was moving across a field. "What's that?" he asked.

"Oh wow!" Xena cried. "It's a flock of sheep with one of those herding dogs! I've always wanted to see that!"

Their father stopped the car, and for a while they sat and watched the beautiful black and white dog cleverly maneuvering sheep down the field and through a narrow gate into a paddock. As the shepherd passed near them he raised his hand briefly in greeting. In a moment the sheep went over a low rise and out of sight, and their father started up the engine and they drove off.

They drove farther on and got out of the car and climbed enormous piles of rocks, speckled with moss and lichen, which the guidebook said were the foundations of an ancient Druidic temple. They ate their picnic perched on the ruins and went back to exploring.

All day long, though, Xena and Xander couldn't stop thinking about the Beast. As they climbed around the huge rocks of the temple, Xena was thinking, I wonder what kind of creature could make that weird footprint Sherlock drew in his notebook. She kept her eyes peeled for a footprint, a tuft of fur, a broken branch, anything out of the ordinary.

Xander was thinking, There's got to be a way to solve this case without an actual Beast encounter. He scanned the countryside from the highest rock, hoping for a long-distance glimpse of something large and brown and shaggy. He couldn't help feeling they were getting close to something scary. Every shadow made him jump, and once, when a hawk shrieked in the air above him, he nearly fell off the rocks he was clambering over.

"Boy, I'm tired," their mom said as she climbed into the car at the end of the day. "Let's get back and see if Mrs. Roberts has any coffee in the kitchen. Tea's fine, but . . ."

Xander relaxed with relief. He wasn't going to have to confront the Beast after all—at least not today.

"But, Mom," Xena said, "you said we could go to the woods. We haven't seen anything wild today." *Shut up*, Xander thought.

"Except for that spider that went down your shirt," their dad said, steering around a rut in the road. "I don't know which was wilder, you or the spider! I haven't seen you hop around like that in a long time."

Xena *had* looked pretty funny when she felt all those legs tickling down the back of her neck. Xander would remember that the next time she teased him about his fear of wild animals. At least he didn't screech at a harmless little spider.

"You *promised*," Xena said.

"We didn't promise," their father said.

He's so unfair sometimes, she thought. That was practically a promise. And we were on his side about going for a hike instead of to the sale preview!

"And we're tired," their mom said. "We'll have plenty of chances to go exploring tomorrow. There's a walking tour of local sites of interest tomorrow morning. How does that sound?"

Xena and Xander looked at each other. Boring, each could almost hear the other thinking. And they were nearly at the woods. If a beast was hiding—and howling—around here, it was probably living among the shadows of the trees, Xander thought. Otherwise people would have seen it, wouldn't they?

A few small clouds were making soft streaks across the sky. "Ooh, that's so pretty," their mom said. "Can you pull over for a minute? I want to take some pictures. The manor house we just passed is so pretty in this light, and the clouds are gorgeous."

"I thought you were in a hurry to get back," their father said. He slowed down the car and put on the blinker.

"I was. But those clouds! It will just take a minute."

They all got out, and Mrs. Holmes leaned against the fence that ran along the road, taking picture after picture. "Let's wait a few minutes and see if they change their shape," she said. "It's so peaceful here."

"Can I take one?" Xander asked. His mom handed him the camera, and he pointed it toward the sky, keeping some of the dark trees in the foreground for contrast. Cool, he thought, and moved a few steps away to get a different angle.

Xena hopped over the waist-high fence—it was easy since the track coach at school had been training her on hurdles—and started looking at the ground. "Coming, Xander?" He shook his head. "Mom and Dad are right here," she reminded him. "We won't go far."

"I'm taking pictures."

"Oh, all *right*." As she moved away from him, she muttered just loud enough for him to hear, "What a baby."

Xena soon found herself getting farther and farther away from her family. She could still see the car and hear her parents' voices. But the woods were thicker than they looked from the road, and it was dark in there. It would be a good place for something to hide. Even something big could stay out of sight here. Something big, with sharp claws and enough strength to break a fence. Xena started at a sound, but it was just a squirrel scrambling up a tree.

She was about to turn back when something caught her eye. One of the tree's branches was broken. The break was above her head. Xena was already almost as tall as her mom, so whoever—or whatever—had hit the branch with enough force to snap it must have been as tall as a man. Maybe it was a man, she told herself.

She inspected the break. It looked pretty new; the splinters along the edge were still sharp and hadn't been worn down by exposure to wind and rain. And there, just past it, was another broken branch.

She glanced down and saw something else. She squatted. Was that a footprint? It was about the right length but broader than a footprint should be, and were those toe-marks or just depressions in the dirt? It was too dark in the thick trees to be sure.

Xena stood up. "Xander!" she called. "Could you come here?"

A few moments later he pushed through the trees. "Are you sure you want a *baby* with you?"

"Sorry," Xena said. "I didn't mean—sorry."

"Anyway, what do you want?" He glanced back toward the road. It had been hard for him to go into the woods, but he'd proved his point to Xena. Now he'd do whatever it was she wanted and get back to the car before the sun set any further.

Xena pointed at the ground, and Xander bent over, his hands on his knees. "Hmm." He pulled the shiny camera out of his pocket.

"Great idea!" She reached for it. The camera's flash would illuminate the footprint, or whatever it was.

"No way. I thought of it."

"Well, I found the footprint," she said, but she cared more about getting the picture than about being the one to take it, so she moved to the side.

Xander snapped the picture, the white flash lighting up the scene. He took two more for good measure.

"Xena!" It was their dad. "Xander!"

"Coming!" they called together and headed back to the car. Then Xander pulled up short and Xena nearly ran into him.

"Watch out!" she said, but he just pointed at the fence.

"Look." One whole section was fresh new wood, and sawdust lay under it. "Someone recently repaired it. This must be where it was broken!"

"Duh," Xena said. "Let's—"

"Come on!" Their father sounded impatient, so Xander snapped a quick shot of the fence, and they ran back to the car.

"Did you get your picture?" their mom said as their dad pulled back onto the road.

"Just a sec." Xena pressed the buttons to show the last pictures taken. She nudged Xander. "Take a look at this!" she whispered.

"I can't. I'll get sick."

"Oh, right."

"Well, what is it?" he asked impatiently as she stared at the camera in silence.

"It's the footprint." Her hushed voice was high with excitement. "A huge footprint, and it has only four toes—just like the one in the case-book!"

Xander's voice cracked as he said, "Then . . . then the Beast is *real*."

Xena nodded. All she felt was excitement, but in Xander excitement mingled with fear until he felt like he was going to throw up.

CHAPTER 9

Their mother reached back her hand for the camera. "I want to see how those cloud pictures came out."

"Just one more second, Mom," Xena pleaded. She clicked the button back a frame and saw that this picture was even clearer. There was no doubt about it: a big flat-footed footprint with a missing toe. There was also a shot of the repaired fence. She passed the camera forward.

"Any good ones?" their dad asked, and while their parents discussed the photos, Xena and Xander leaned in toward each other to talk about what they had found.

"The footprint looked just the same as the one Sherlock drew in the notebook," Xena said. "And the branch above it was broken, really high up, like by something tall."

Xander shut his eyes, picturing the eerie creature Sherlock had drawn and imagining it tall enough to break that high branch. "It's the Beast," he said. "It's got to be."

"Well, it was *something* big," Xena conceded.

He swallowed hard, fighting back his fear. He was Sherlock Holmes's descendant, and he wanted to solve this case. He couldn't give up now. Maybe he just needed a little of Xena's skeptical approach. "Okay," he said, sounding calmer than he felt. "All we know for sure is that something big is out there. Now we have to come up with our next step."

They fell into silence for the rest of the ride, trying to think what they should do next.

There was a lot of interesting material in the library, Xander thought. We should definitely go back there.

I can't wait to get out in the woods again and see what else we can find! ran through Xena's mind.

As they pulled up at the B and B, Mrs. Roberts came out and stood in the doorway, wiping her hands on her apron. "Just in time for supper! Would you like to join us?"

"That's very nice of you," their mother said. "We're all hungry."

Again, Mrs. Roberts had made sandwiches. "Out in the country we stick to the old-fashioned ways. Our big meal is at midday, and we have our tea in the late afternoon. So it's just sandwiches since nobody's very hungry at suppertime as a rule."

They sat down and dug in. Mr. and Mrs. Roberts kept glancing at the door and then at the clock on the wall.

At home, the sandwiches would have been peanut butter and jelly or maybe tuna fish. Here, there were all sorts of interesting new things to try: egg and olive, cucumber slices with lots of butter on brown bread, and a tender green leaf that Mr. Roberts called watercress. They sampled each of them. Xander wasn't crazy about the egg and olive, but the others were really good. Xena ate some of everything.

"These are delicious," their mother said.

Mrs. Roberts blushed. "Cooking's in my blood, I think," she said modestly.

The back door opened and then banged shut, and Mrs. Roberts looked up with her lips pressed together. Is she angry at something? Xena wondered.

Trevor came into the room. "Sorry I'm late," he mumbled as he pulled a chair up to the table.

"Young man," Mr. Roberts said. "You know the rules. Home before dark."

"The sun's just setting now!" Trevor protested.

This seemed a little odd to Xena. Blackslope was such a peaceful little town. Why would a boy Xander's age have to be home so early? Were the Robertses overprotective grandparents? Or could they be anxious because they knew that the Beast was around?

Trevor ate sandwich after sandwich with his head down, and in just a few minutes he pushed back from the table. "May I go spend the night at Ian's house?"

"Of course not," his grandmother answered.

"You know the rules," Mr. Roberts said again.

"I have the rental car right outside," Mr. Holmes broke in. "I'd be happy to drive Trevor to his friend's house."

Trevor brightened and said, "Thanks!" but Mrs. Roberts said, "You're too kind, but Trevor has to stay in tonight." Trevor scowled and stomped out of the room.

"I'm so sorry," Mrs. Roberts said, and their mother said, "Oh, we know how it is with kids! Why don't you two go relax? We'll clean up."

"I bet Trevor's being grounded for something," Xander said after the kitchen had been tidied up. He and Xena were in the sitting room, playing a card game and waiting for their chance to get to work on the case.

"Probably," Xena said. This *was* the most likely explanation for the Robertses' behavior, but she wasn't convinced. They had seemed more worried than angry.

Their mom poked her head into the sitting room. "We're going up to bed. You kids ran us ragged today! Don't be too late, okay?"

"Okay," said Xander.

Xena called out, "Good night."

When their parents were safely upstairs Xander said, "Finally! Now we can put all our evidence together." He pulled a tuft of woolly material from his pocket.

"Whoa!" Xena snatched it up. "Where did you get that from? And why didn't you show me until now?"

"Some fell off the table when that guy in the library picked it up." Xander was smug. "I grabbed it. And it's not like we had a chance to examine it in private until now!" Actually, he had been hoping for an impressed reaction if he kept his find a surprise, and it had worked.

Xena was examining the fluffy material, her head tilted to one side. Something was odd about it. But what? Then it hit her. "Check this out, Xander. When blood dries, it turns brown. The blood on this wool is still bright red, even though it was found this morning."

"You mean . . . ?" Xander looked at her with raised eyebrows.

"Maybe it isn't really blood. If it was real, wouldn't it have turned brown by now?"

"How do you know sheep blood acts the same as human blood? Maybe sheep blood doesn't turn brown," Xander pointed out.

A noise behind them made them look up. Xander caught sight of Trevor peering into the room. "'Night," he mumbled when Xander smiled at him. He headed up the stairs.

"How come everyone in this town goes to bed so early?" Xander wanted to know. "Even the kids on a school holiday week?"

But there was nothing else to do, so they went upstairs too. It took Xena a long time to fall asleep. Every time she started to doze off, some creak or crackle in the house would zing through her and wake her up. And when she finally did fall into a restless sleep, she was awakened by the sound of footsteps. She flopped over and pulled the pillow over her head.

Then she pulled it off and sat up. Now that

she was more awake and thought about it, she realized something.

The footsteps were coming from outside.

She went to her window and pulled the curtain aside. Almost immediately she jumped back again. It was still dark, but there was no mistaking what she'd seen. A huge shaggy figure stood directly under her window, hunched over, enormous paws pushing aside the shrubbery.

Without stopping to think, Xena tore through the hall and down the stairs. She threw the door open and looked out.

Nothing. Disappointment nearly choked her.

Then something brushed against her arm.

CHAPTER 10

Yee-OW!" Xena yelled, and she leaped a foot in the air.

"Chill!" It was Xander. "It's only me. Sorry I scared you," he added hastily as she glowered at him. "I just wanted to get your attention without making any noise. But you blew it."

"Well, how was I to know it was you?" Xena's heart was pounding so hard it made her teeth click. "And you didn't scare me—you startled me. There's a difference." She waited for her heart to stop thumping, then asked, "Why did you come down here? Did you see something?"

"I heard something," Xander said. "It sounded like someone was walking around outside."

"I heard it too," she said, and told him what she'd seen.

Xander looked out at the inky blackness. Without streetlights, hardly anything was visible. And he couldn't imagine that anything—human or animal—would stick around after Xena's scream.

Xena sighed. "Let's look for footprints as soon as it's light tomorrow morning."

They went back inside, Xena reluctantly, Xander glad that she wasn't going to pressure him into investigating a wild beast in the dark. But before they reached the stairs a light snapped on. They froze. Busted!

"Uh-oh," Xena said.

Mr. and Mrs. Roberts were standing on the landing halfway down the stairway, looking grim. "What are you children doing?" Mrs. Roberts demanded. "Why did you open the door? Don't you know it's dange—"

"Hush, dear," Mr. Roberts said.

"I saw something under my window," Xena said. "It wasn't a person. It was bigger than a person, and it looked like it was covered with fur."

Mrs. Roberts went white, even to her lips. She clung to her husband. "Oh, Nigel." Her voice was barely audible. "Oh, Nigel, it's the Beast. It's back."

Xander felt his heart sink. So it was true! Whatever was causing all this uproar wasn't a person. It was some kind of wild creature.

"The Beast?" Xena asked eagerly. Now they

were getting somewhere! "You mean the Beast from a hundred years ago?"

Mr. Roberts answered quickly as though to prevent his wife from speaking. "We mean nothing of the sort. Now scoot back up to bed."

They didn't exactly scoot, but they went upstairs. Xander shot a glance at Trevor's door as he went past it. It was shut tight. He must be a heavy sleeper, he thought.

And they didn't exactly go to sleep either. At least not for a long time.

Xena stood outside her bedroom window the next morning, hands on her hips, peering at the ground.

"What's the matter?" Xander joined her. The smooth lawn with well-trimmed shrubbery looked so calm in the daylight. A brick walkway with a white metal workbench in the middle led through a tidy little flower bed.

But Xena wasn't admiring the garden. "Gravel," she said in disgust. "It goes all the way up to the house on this side. And it's dry. You can't even tell if anything stood there, much less the shape of its foot."

Xander squatted. There was no sign of the Beast here. He felt a mixture of disappointment and relief. "Cheer up. The thing you saw had to come from somewhere. Sure it wasn't this bush that you were looking at?"

"Positive. It was lots bigger and shaggy. And it was moving, like it was pushing its way through the bush. Do you think I'm imagining things? Or dreaming?"

"Okay, okay," Xander said. "Chill. I'm just trying to make sure."

"Make sure of what?"

He didn't answer and she was too cranky from lack of sleep to pursue it. They walked around the area slowly, bent over with their eyes on the ground, trying to find a footprint, some flattened grass, broken twigs—anything that would tell them which direction the Beast had come from.

"Nothing," Xander said. "I bet it hasn't rained here in a week. The ground's hard, and the grass just bounces back after you step on it." He pressed his foot into the ground and lifted it up to demonstrate. Sure enough, the neatly trimmed grass sprang right back. "What's the point of being in this wet country if it stops raining just when you need clues?"

Xena didn't answer right away.

"I said what's the point—"

"Xander, come here. I think I've found something! Look at this!" She was pointing at the top of a wooden frame that supported a climbing rosebush.

At first he didn't see anything. Then—"Wow!" Xander couldn't help being intrigued. "Could that be a piece of fur?" Something was stuck in a broken place at the top of one of the posts. He stretched one hand up but the clump of fuzz was way out of his reach.

"Wait a sec," Xena said. "We have to do it carefully. We need to preserve the evidence."

Xander hung back, letting his sister shinny expertly up the sturdy post. The fingers of her right hand removed the dark brown clump while she held on with her left. In a moment she dropped lightly down to the ground and held out her palm to her brother.

"Sure looks like fur," she said.

Xander nodded. Despite his worry about coming face-to-face with a wild animal, he was starting to get excited and to think like a detective. They had a solid clue now, and they had to figure out what it meant. "It's too fuzzy to be human hair. And it's too high up to be from a dog, even a really big one. I haven't seen any big dogs around here, have you?"

Xena shook her head. "And all the sheep we've seen are white, so it can't be some wool that floated up there somehow. Remember what Sherlock always said." Together they recited, "'When you have excluded the impossible, whatever remains, however improbable, must be the truth.'"

"We've excluded humans and dogs and sheep, so even though a beast is improbable, it's the only explanation left," Xander said. "And we've got good solid evidence too. Nobody could say that this was a dream! Let's send it to the SPFD. Maybe the lab can analyze it."

At the stationer's on the village square they found a puffy envelope. Xena addressed it to Andrew Watson, the boy at the Society for the Preservation of Famous Detectives who had shown them around the SPFD's lab. Before she sealed the envelope, Xander pulled the MP3 player out of his pocket. He hated to have to go without music for the rest of the vacation, but it would be a small sacrifice if the lab could analyze the roar of the Beast as well as its fur.

When they mailed the package (overnight so that Andrew would get right on it), the clerk behind the counter said, "You're the kids who're staying at the Robertses' place, right?" Xena said they were, and the clerk pulled out a bundle of letters. "Would you mind giving these letters to Mrs. Roberts? Save the postman a few steps."

"Sure." Xander took the bundle of mail. He glanced at the top letter and caught his breath.

"Zee," he said, "do you know what Mrs. Roberts's first name is?"

Xena's eyebrows drew together as she thought back. "I heard her husband call her Lina a couple of times. Why?"

"Lina must be a nickname." Xander held out the letter.

Xena read, "'Mrs. Adeline Roberts.'" Then she looked at Xander. "So?"

"Adeline is the name of the lady Mr. Tuttle told us about, the one who disappeared."

"So?"

"Mrs. Roberts has the same name, or almost, and she says cooking is in her blood. Adeline was a cook. And I just remembered! That picture in Mr. Tuttle's book—remember? It seemed familiar to me and now I know why. It looks *just* like the picture on the mantelpiece inside. Don't you see? The cook who disappeared must be Mrs. Roberts's great-great-grandmother! I think it's time we talked to Mr. and Mrs. Roberts."

"I'll let you do the talking," Xena said. "Flash

those dimples!" He gave her a phony smile and they both cracked up, their earlier irritation forgotten in the triumph of their discovery.

They found Mrs. Roberts reading the paper in the kitchen. Xander gave her the letters from the clerk. "Mrs. Roberts," he said carefully, "we were wondering about your first name."

She looked up at him in surprise. "What were you wondering?"

"If you were named for that other Adeline," Xander went on. "The one who disappeared."

Mrs. Roberts went white again. "How could you possibly know about that?"

"Our great-great-great-grandfather, Sherlock Holmes, came here a century ago to investigate the Beast of Blackslope," Xena explained.

To their surprise Mrs. Roberts burst into tears. Xena got her a glass of water and a dish towel to wipe her eyes with, and Xander stood by awkwardly, wondering what they had said to upset her.

"Are you okay?" he asked when her sobs slowed down.

"I am so sorry, children," she said. "It's just that . . ." She swallowed and dabbed at her eyes with the towel.

Mr. Roberts's voice came from the doorway.

"Here, what's this?" He hurried in. "What is it, my dear?"

She smiled shakily up at him. "These children are the descendants of Sherlock Holmes. But even he couldn't help."

"Help with *what*?" Xena felt like she was going to burst if nobody said anything directly. "Do you mean to say that the Beast is back?"

Mrs. Roberts nodded. "Either that, or it never went away."

"Is that why you've been—" Xena hesitated. She didn't want to be rude. "Is that why you haven't been sleeping well?"

"Lina—" Mr. Roberts said, but she kept going, her voice high and rapid.

"There's a curse on my family, you see. Every fourth or fifth generation in my family, someone disappears in the most awful way. Two hundred years ago an ancestor of mine, a doctor, set off at night from the Chimington estate to tend a man in the village who was sick with fever. People reported hearing mysterious howls that night, and the doctor was never seen again. A hundred years later the Beast carried off my great-great-grandmother, and now it's back. And that means it's come for me. Or even worse—for Trevor."

CHAPTER 11

Mrs. Roberts looked so sad and scared. Xena reached out and touched the woman's arm. "Don't worry," she said. Xena wished she knew how to reassure her. How dare anything—or anyone—frighten a nice old lady like that?

"Is that why you wouldn't let Trevor go out after dark?" Xander asked.

"Yes," Mr. Roberts said. "The mayor has suggested that everyone stay inside after sundown. It's not really a curfew—the town doesn't have the power to do something so drastic without involving more authorities, and nobody in Blackslope wants word of the Beast to get out. They don't want to risk chasing tourists away if it turns out to be nothing." Then he gave them a curious look. "How do you know about Sherlock Holmes coming here to investigate the Beast?"

"We inherited one of his journals," Xander

explained. "He has some notes about the investigation in it."

"Do you think Sherlock Holmes found out anything that would help?" Mrs. Roberts asked. She seemed more composed now.

"He had to give up," Xena admitted, and the old lady's face fell. Xena and Xander looked at each other, more determined than ever to solve the case.

After breakfast Xena and Xander were sitting at the cleared table with pens, paper, and Sherlock Holmes's casebook.

"Let's get organized about this," Xena said. She pulled the paper and pen toward her. Under POSSIBILITIES, she drew a line to make two columns. The first was headed *The Beast of Blackslope has returned or it never went away,* and the second *Someone is trying to make people believe the Beast of Blackslope has returned.*

"I think the second is more likely," Xena said. "Someone is going around leaving footprints and bits of wool and stuff, howling, maybe even wearing a costume."

Xander cheered up at the thought. "Who would do that? And why?"

"Let's do why first. Maybe that will help us figure out the who."

"Motive," she wrote.

To scare people

To scare one specific person—Mrs. Roberts?

"What about money?" Xander suggested. "Money is a pretty common motive. Maybe someone is making money from pretending there really is a Beast."

Xena shrugged. "I don't see how. Mrs. Roberts says everyone in town is afraid the Beast will scare tourists away. That means no money." Still, she added another motive: *Money.*

"Okay, that's all the whys I can think of." Xena nibbled the end of the pen. "Now let's work on the who."

Neither could come up with anyone who would want to scare someone. "Well then, who could make money from this?" Xena frowned in concentration.

"Mr. Tuttle, maybe?" Xander suggested. "He'd sell more books if people got interested in the Beast."

"I don't see how he could do all that from a wheelchair—make footprints and break fences and all."

"Unless he's just pretending to need a wheelchair. Or maybe he has an accomplice working with him!"

"True," Xena admitted. "Still, it seems like an awfully complicated way to sell some books, and it doesn't seem to be working. What now?"

"How about those pictures we took?"

"Good idea," Xena said, and she disappeared. She came back five minutes later with their mother's camera. "Let's compare the picture of the footprint with Sherlock's drawing." She turned on the camera and clicked through the photographs of Xander clowning around on top of a rock, of a clump of wildflowers, of herself with her mouth full of potato salad. That was the last one. No footprints.

She went to the doorway. "Mom!" she called out into the hall. "What happened to the pictures I took yesterday?"

Her mother called back, "What pictures? Oh, you mean those ones in the woods? Honey, I didn't think you wanted to save those. They looked like they didn't come out. Did you really want to save pictures of dirt and a fence?"

"Yes! Oh, Mom, you don't mean you erased them, do you?"

"Sorry. I did it this morning so I'd have more room for pictures today."

Xena groaned. "Xander, you do remember what the pictures looked like, don't you?"

"I didn't see them. Remember? I would have puked."

Xena tried to remember. It had been getting dark and the car was moving, but even so she thought she had seen clearly enough that the footprint in the woods had looked like the one in Sherlock's journal. But she could no longer be sure. Why did the one with the photographic memory also have to be the one who got carsick?

She swallowed her disappointment. "Well, what else does it say in the notebook?"

Xander studied the page. "Just stuff we read already. The kind of thing the Beast was doing back then sounds a lot like what's going on now. Sherlock wrote that he was asked here by Lord Chimington, and he stayed at Blackslope Manor as a guest when he came with Dr. Watson to investigate." He looked up. "Not a whole lot to go on, is it?"

"No, it's not. But there's something there anyway." Xena tapped her lips with the end of the pen, thinking. "That footprint in the woods was right near Blackslope Manor, wasn't it? Remember, Mom said something about the manor right before we stopped. And it sounded like the howls came from there, and Adeline the cook and her mean husband lived behind the stable there. We need to go to the manor and poke around a bit and see what we can find."

Xander thought back to the day before. "What about that pre-auction viewing thing Mom was talking about? Isn't the auction *at* Blackslope Manor?" The thought of not having to go back into the woods was a huge relief.

They went downstairs and found their parents in the sitting room.

"Mom," Xander said, sitting on the arm of her big overstuffed chair, "we did what Dad wanted yesterday, so let's do what you want today. Is that pre-auction viewing going on?"

"Well, how sweet." Their mother gave him a hug. "But are you sure you want to do that?"

"We're sure," Xena said.

"Fine with me," their father said. "Let's go!"

Xander ran back upstairs for the cold-case notebook. He gave it to Xena, who stuffed it in her backpack. They jumped into the car.

Xena looked out the window as they drove toward the manor. Hills rolled away on both sides of the road, some dotted with sheep. The hedges were thick but not threatening, and the stand of trees where they had found the foot-print looked a lot smaller than it had seemed last night. She thought of asking their parents to stop so that they could take another picture, but she didn't want to face the questions this would bring. Maybe on the way back she'd think of an excuse to check it out again.

"It's hard to picture a creature hiding out in those woods," she said to Xander. "They're so pretty, not the kind of place where a wild animal would live."

"I guess," Xander said. The problem was, he could picture a wild creature hiding just about anywhere. What if they found it—and it went after him or Xena? How could they possibly fight a monster like that?

"Wow!" Xena said as the magnificent old house came into view. The car turned into a drive that went down a gentle slope and then rose again to the house in a huge circular sweep. Lofty columns ran along the front of the graceful stone building, and many of the large windows were open in the warm morning, showing white curtains that flapped in the breeze.

"Can't you just imagine carriages coming up to this door for a ball?" she asked.

"Or people getting ready to go out on a fox hunt?" Xander said.

"Yuck," said Xena. "Poor little fox."

"Poor little fox, nothing," their father said

from the front seat. "They carry disease and they kill people's pets. They even have them in London now."

A dozen or so cars were already parked by the house. Hand-lettered signs reading PREVIEW THIS WAY pointed left.

"You kids coming?" their mother asked as she got out.

Xander started after her but Xena pulled him back and asked hastily, "Can we go exploring?" Their mother looked doubtful, so Xena added, "It's such a nice day." Xander started to object but changed his mind. This was a regular old country house with sheep and probably with dogs. No wild animals were likely to be around.

"All right," their father said. "Just keep out of mischief, okay?"

They followed the flagstone walkway to the right, around to the back of the house. "Can you imagine living in a place like this?" Xena asked.

Xander shook his head, craning his neck to gaze at the upper stories. "You could spend weeks exploring. They must have lots of servants."

Xena stumbled on a broken flagstone and said, "Well, I hope they take better care of the house than the garden. Look at this place."

They stopped and surveyed the lawn. It was

a mess, with uncut grass and overgrown shrubbery. Wildflowers and weeds competed for space with plants that looked as if they had been carefully chosen long ago. A rusty rake and a broken watering can leaned against a bush.

"You can tell that used to be a maze." Xander pointed at ragged hedges that still preserved some of the angles and openings that must have once made a puzzle. "And look at this building." He climbed the steps of a forlorn gazebo whose roof gaped with holes and whose floor had moss creeping over it. He sat down on a bench and hastily stood up again when it creaked as though it was about to break.

"What is it, a hexagon?" Xena put her hands on her hips and looked up at the ceiling. She counted the sides. "No, an octagon. Must have been pretty once." She looked at the faded paint that could have been yellow years ago.

"Did you say octagon?" Xander asked. Xena nodded and started down the steps. "Wait a sec, Zee. Let me see the notebook."

Xena stopped and pulled the straps of her backpack off her shoulders, and then rummaged around in it. She handed the book to her brother.

Xander leafed through it. "Aha!" He was triumphant. "Check it out!"

"Whoa!" she said. "A drawing of an octagon! I didn't even notice that before. Do you think it's this building?"

"Could be." Xander was starting to get excited. "Look! It is! This big rectangle with lots of lines in it is this house. It looks just like those architectural drawings that contractor guy made when Mom and Dad were talking about putting an addition on the kitchen back home, remember?"

"Yes!" Xena pointed at the drawing. "There's the front porch with the columns, and the big circular drive. Xander! Remember that Sherlock said he stayed at the manor when he came to investigate the Beast? It looks like he didn't just sleep here—he must have thought there was something important about the house and the barn and things. That's why he drew the map of the manor!"

Xander read, " 'Invited to Blackslope Manor, home of Lord Chimington. V. good dinner, hard bed. Interesting.'" He looked up. "Interesting what? I wonder."

"Not the dinner, I guess. Or the hard bed. Does he say any more?"

Xander studied the page. "Nothing more about what was interesting, if that's what you

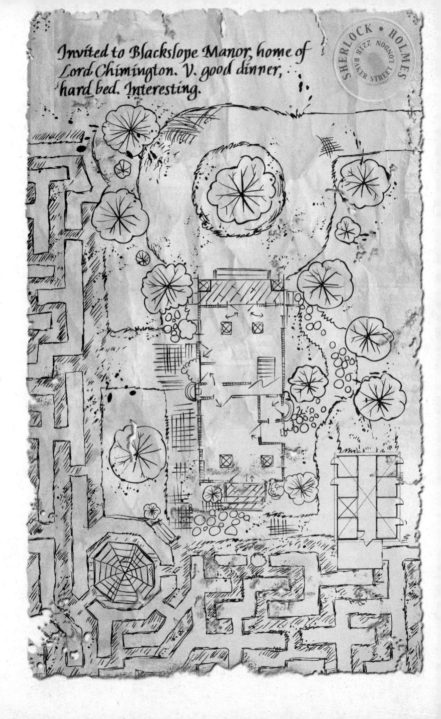

Invited to Blackslope Manor, home of
Lord Chimington. V. good dinner,
hard bed. Interesting.

SHERLOCK · HOLMES
BIZZ NOONOT
BAKER STREET

mean. But what's this weird-looking shape supposed to be?"

"Let me look." Xena turned the page so that it was facing her and studied it. "Those aren't regular rooms. See? No doors. It's like a bunch of closets lined up in a row." She thought another minute. "Don't you think it looks like a stable? Those lines could mark where the stalls for the horses are! And Adeline and her husband lived in an addition built onto the stable, remember? I wonder if it's still here."

Xander rose to his feet and put the book back in Xena's pack. "Let's figure this out. This property is *huge* and we don't have time to look all over. Mom and Dad won't take too long at the pre-auction thing, so we have to work fast. If there's a stable, where would it be?"

Xena tried to imagine what the manor would have looked like in the old days, before there were cars. "In Sherlock's time, they would have driven their carriages up to the front door, right?"

"Right! And that drive is long but not too wide, so the coachmen probably didn't turn the carriages around but just kept going straight and put them away after the people got out."

"So the stable must be on the other side of

the house from where Dad parked," Xena said. "Let's go!"

She took off running, and even wearing the pack, she outdistanced Xander easily. "Slow down!" he called, but she disappeared. When he caught up to her she was standing triumphantly at the door to a large wooden building that was painted brown. "Why do you keep doing that?" He was exasperated. "You shouldn't ditch me like that."

But she ignored him. "Look at this. I bet this is the place!" The door was enormous, easily large enough to lead in two horses side by side. It had to be the stable. Was the place where the cook and her husband lived still there? Where should they start looking?

"Did you try the door?" Xander asked.

She shook her head. "I was waiting for you."

"Thanks." He reached out his hand.

Just then a deep voice behind them said, "What are you kids doing here?"

CHAPTER 12

Xena and Xander whipped around, their hearts thumping.

A man, his bushy gray eyebrows drawn together in a frown, stood a few feet away. He was leaning on a cane and glaring at them. "I said, what are you kids doing here?" the man repeated. "This part of the grounds isn't open to the public."

"Oh—w-we didn't know," Xena stammered. "Our parents were looking at, you know, the antiques, and we—"

"We were getting bored, sir." Xander managed to appear younger than his ten years as he looked up through his long dark eyelashes. "We didn't mean to get in the way, but our parents have been looking at the antiques for *hours* and we wanted to take a walk."

"Well," the old man said, still gruffly but with less menace, "since you're here with your parents, let's go find them and see what they have to say."

Just then Xena and Xander heard a sneeze. A boy about Xena's age came around the corner of the stable. "It's all right, Mr. Whittaker," he told the old man.

"Do you know these children, Master Ian?"

"Of course. They're Xena and Xander Holmes. Americans. They're here for the holidays, just like me."

How did this boy know all that? News must really get around in the small town.

"As long as they're friends of yours," the old man grumbled, and without saying good-bye he turned and went off, leaning heavily on his cane. He stopped at a bend in the walkway and called back, "Just don't let them in that stable!"

When he was safely gone Xena said to the boy, "Thanks for the rescue, but who are you?"

Before he could answer, Xander said, "I know! You're the boy from London!"

The boy—Ian—looked baffled. "How did you know I'm from London?" He sneezed again.

"Oh, he's *that* one!" Xena said. "I thought he looked familiar!"

"Will one of you please explain what you're talking about?"

"We saw you our first day here," Xander said. "We were in that little park by the B and B we're staying in—"

"The Robertses' place," Ian said, nodding. "Trevor is a friend of mine. He told me about you two."

They explained about the Game and about spotting the transit pass sticking out of his pocket. Xena almost told him about seeing him trip on the sidewalk, but she decided it would be rude. Nobody likes to be noticed being a klutz.

"Very clever!" Ian said with a laugh. "But I don't always live in London. I go to boarding school there, and I come home to Blackslope Manor on holidays and in the summer."

"You live *here*? In the manor house?" Xena couldn't imagine actually living in this great big place.

"Oh, it's nice enough." Ian kicked the gravel. "But it's dull here. And the house is falling down. I'd rather be in London any day."

"Why was that old man so angry?" Xander asked.

"He wasn't really angry. He just sees the stable and the grounds as his own personal property."

"Why? Is he some kind of relative?" Xena wondered.

Ian shook his head. "No, although in a way he might as well be. Mr. Whittaker's the caretaker. His family have been with the Blackslopes for generations."

"I thought you were the Chimingtons." Xena was bewildered.

"I know it's confusing. Our surname is Blackslope but the title is Chimington. My father is George Blackslope, Lord Chimington. See?" They didn't really, but they knew that in England titles were pretty important to a lot of people, so they nodded.

Ian frowned thoughtfully. "Mr. Whittaker's the last one of his line, though. The Whittakers never had any children." He went on as if he was talking to himself. "Soon there will be no more Blackslopes and no more Whittakers at Blackslope Manor." Then he seemed to remember that he wasn't alone, and he smiled brightly at Xena and Xander. "That will make everything easier for me. My mother will quit her job at the tourist agency, my parents will move into a flat in London, and I won't have to take the train home on holidays. Home will be right there on the Tube line!"

"Yes, but . . ." Xander didn't like to leave a question until he got the answer to it. "But why was Mr. Whittaker angry? We weren't doing anything."

"Oh, he's just suspicious. He breeds dogs and he has a litter of puppies in there." Ian nodded at the door of the stable. "He's always convinced some other breeder is going to send spies to see his dogs, for some reason." He laughed. "I can't imagine what harm a spy could do, but he's a little batty on the subject. And anyway, he's even grumpier than usual these days. He's not looking forward to leaving the manor, even though my parents are buying him a nice cottage close to town."

"Hey, I bet you know all about the story of the Beast of Blackslope," Xander said, "since a lot of it happened right here."

Ian blinked. "The Beast? What do you know about that?"

Xena and Xander told him what they'd read in Sherlock's casebook, and what Mr. Tuttle had told them, that he believed the Beast was back.

"Or maybe it never left," Ian said. "It's true what Mr. Tuttle said about the cook disappearing. He knows a lot about the Beast. But not everything."

"What do you mean?" Xander asked.

"This isn't the first time it's reappeared. It

carried off my uncle Philip when he was a teenager."

"*What?*" Xena and Xander couldn't believe that no one had mentioned this before. Xander felt his stomach turn over at the thought of someone being carried off by the Beast.

Ian nodded. "He just disappeared one day. All they ever found were huge footprints. And his jacket. I still have it."

"Wow!" Xena said. "What else?"

"Nothing." Ian shrugged. "There were no more clues. No one ever heard from Philip again. And there've been other strange disappearances."

Just then they heard a woman's voice calling Ian's name.

"Got to run!" Ian said. "Maybe I'll see you in the village before you leave." He turned and tripped over a garden hoe that was lying right out in plain view. Xena ran to help him, but he got up, brushed off his knees, and said, "Don't worry! I'm all right," and limped away.

They watched him go, too surprised to speak for a moment.

"Well!" Xena finally said. "It looks like we have some more investigating to do."

"Definitely," her brother agreed. "There's

something here that doesn't add up. Mrs. Roberts said it was *her* family that was cursed, not the Blackslopes. And neither she nor Mr. Tuttle mentioned Ian's uncle. Let's find Mom and Dad and see if they can take us to the library." He turned back toward the house. "I want to find out more about this missing Uncle Philip."

They went in through the manor's front door, entering a huge high-ceilinged room. The house seemed to be filled with people walking around holding pamphlets. Everywhere Xena and Xander looked they saw shining wood tables heaped with china, silver, books, and paintings. Each item had a sticker with a number written on it. "How will we ever find Mom and Dad?" Xander asked.

"Just start looking, I guess. Let's split up. We'll meet back at the front door."

Xander went to the left down a long corridor with a suit of armor standing in a niche, and Xena turned into a smaller room where even the cushions on the sofa had stickers on them. How sad, she thought, imagining how she would feel if everything her family owned was going to be sold. She didn't see her parents in there, but she did briefly meet Ian's mom, who looked a lot like

Ian. Xena introduced herself and then moved on to the next room. She was about to give up and follow in the direction Xander had taken when suddenly she saw him waving at her from a doorway.

She managed to get through the crowd to where he stood. "Find them?"

"No," Xander said, "but I did find something *very* interesting."

"What?"

"Ian lied to us. His uncle Philip wasn't carried off by the Beast or anything else!"

CHAPTER 13

For a minute Xena could only stare at Xander. "What do you mean, Ian's uncle wasn't carried off by the Beast?"

"Come with me!" Xander disappeared into the corridor, and for a moment she lost him. When she caught up with him she saw that he was standing in front of a framed poster. It was a painting of a man with long flowing hair, a mustache, flared pants, and a loose flowered shirt. He was playing a guitar. The colors were all bright—hot pink, turquoise, yellow-green.

"So?" Xena couldn't see the point.

"Look!" Xander gestured to the loopy lettering along the bottom. *Philip and the Philistines*, it read.

"What's a Philistine?" Xena asked, but before Xander could answer she said, "Oh, you think this is his uncle? Oh, come on, Xander—it's not really an unusual name. It could be any Philip."

Xander was shaking his head. "Nuh-uh. There were two men looking at it before, and one said something like, 'The way they acted when Philip ran away to become a rock star, it's surprising they have this poster of him,' and the other said, 'That was the parents. The present Lord Chimington always loved his brother. I'm sure he was very proud of him when he made that album.' Then I asked them if this was Ian's uncle and they said yes."

Xena stood still a moment. "Ian must have been trying to throw us off the trail! That means he knows something. If we see him again, let's not tell him we know he lied, okay?"

"Good idea," Xander agreed. "Let him think he fooled us until we figure out exactly what he's trying to hide."

"Ready to go?" It was their father. He and Mrs. Holmes had come up behind them while they were talking. "We've been looking for you two everywhere!"

On the way back it started pouring, and there was no way they could ask to stop in the woods again. The rain cleared up just as they passed the WELCOME TO BLACKSLOPE sign. "Perfect timing," Xena grumbled under her breath. Then she got an idea. "How about if we go back into town and see if people are talking about the Beast?" she said to Xander. "We need to find out where it's been sighted so we can try to gather more evidence about what it is. That little clump of fur and the howl don't get us very far. Maybe somebody's seen something that could tell us where it hides out when it's not breaking things."

"Sounds like a plan," said Xander. "Could you please drop us in town?" he asked their parents.

"I don't know," their father said. "What about that Beast?"

"Quit teasing, Dad." Xena glanced at her brother. "And anyway, we'll be back before dark."

Their dad pulled over to the side of the road, and Xena and Xander climbed out.

The stores were small and each seemed to specialize in only one thing. One sold knitting supplies, the next sold cookware, and the one past it sold children's clothing. They stepped into every shop and Xena sidled up to anyone she saw engaged in conversation, but she didn't hear anything connected to the Beast.

"Waste of time," Xander grumbled, but Xena said, "Let's try that one." She pointed at a store that looked a bit larger. Xander shrugged and followed her in. It turned out to be a general store that had a little bit of everything—pots and pans and notebooks and clothing and camping gear and garden supplies.

"Hullo," came a voice from behind them. Xena and Xander turned and saw Emma, the blond girl who had been carrying the mysterious black case. Now she was paying for a pack of batteries. "Been touring the area?"

"We went to Blackslope Manor today," Xander told her. "And to the woods near it yesterday."

Emma frowned as she collected her change. "You really ought to try the other end of town. It's a lot more interesting."

"Why?" Xena asked, but the girl just waved at them and hurried out the door.

"What's on the other side of town?" Xena asked her brother.

Xander thought back to the map of Blackslope and all the brochures he had seen. "Just the herb walk. I don't remember anything else being in that direction."

"Strange." Xena shook her head. "Whatever. It's going to get dark soon. I want to try to listen in on one more conversation before we go back to the B and B."

It was fortunate she did, because this time

she got lucky. Two middle-aged women wearing sweaters and squashed-looking hats were standing near the real estate agency, and something about the way they clutched their purses and leaned in close to each other intrigued Xena. She signaled to Xander to stay away.

When she heard one woman say "rustling in the bushes" and "ran all the way home," Xena knew that she had struck gold. She pretended to study the map that showed where the houses for sale were located, and inched closer and closer.

"Right next to where the lane turns in to Gilder's farm," the woman was saying. "I didn't see anything, but what else could be making all that noise?"

"Joseph said he saw something strange down at the bottom of the hill," said the other woman. "That's not too far from there. He said it might have been a cow, but all the fences around there are good and stout. And nobody's reported a missing cow. I think it was the Beast!"

"Oh my," the first woman said. "Seven feet tall, I've heard it was, with horrible long claws and fangs and—"

"Here's our bus," the other one said. The bus pulled up and the two of them stepped on.

Xena reported back to Xander.

"Seven feet tall?" He swallowed. "Let's go back to the B and B."

On the way home Xena remembered that she had run out of shampoo. They stopped at a store that said CHEMIST on the sign (they had learned this was the English way to say drugstore), and the teenage boy who took their money hardly glanced at them. He was too busy talking to a boy with spiked hair who was hanging around the door.

"Someone's going to shoot it," he said. "Mark my words. With the number of hunters around here, it's only a matter of time before someone with a gun will sight it, and that will be that. Old Man Whittaker"—Xena and Xander pricked up their ears at the name—"says that if it comes on the estate again, he's going to take care of it." Xander glanced at Xena, and the clerk seemed to notice them for the first time. He rang up Xena's shampoo. "Anything else?"

"Um, yes," Xena said. "Can you tell me where Gilder's farm is?" He gave her directions. "Thanks," she said.

"Is that where people have seen this Beast?" Xander asked.

"I don't know what you're talking about," said the clerk. The phone rang then, and he picked it up and began to discuss a football match.

"Come on," Xander said. "Let's go look at that map again."

They stopped at the Realtor's window. Xena pressed her finger on the glass. "So here's Gilder's farm." Her finger left a smudge as she moved it to a spot a few inches away. "And I guess this is the lane the lady was talking about. There's only one hill around here that we've seen, so that must be the one, and it's not far from Blackslope Manor. Those guys said that Mr. Whittaker said something about it coming on the estate *again*, so it must have been there already."

"Where was the footprint we found?"

She moved her finger. "There. And here's the B and B."

They studied the map. "So what can we conclude?" Xena asked at last.

"Well," Xander said slowly, "except for a few random times, like when it was near our B and B, all the sightings have been near the manor house. Why do you think that is?"

Xena shrugged. "Maybe there are some good places for it to hide near there?"

"Only one way to find out," Xander said. "We've got to pay another visit to the manor house!"

CHAPTER 14

"What are you two doing here?"

Xena and Xander looked up, startled. It was Trevor, the boy from their B and B, standing on the corner. They had been so absorbed in their conversation they hadn't noticed him. Behind him a young couple stood talking to each other.

"We were just wandering around," Xena said. "It's okay in the daytime, isn't it? Not like at night."

"Oh, and speaking of going out at night," Xander added, "we know why you weren't allowed to go to your friend's house."

"What?" Trevor asked, looking startled at the sudden change of subject. "What do you mean?"

"We heard about the Beast," Xena said. "We know that your grandparents aren't letting you out after dark."

Was it her imagination, she wondered, or did Trevor relax a bit?

"They're pretty overprotective," Trevor said.

"I think that the whole idea of a Beast is silly."

"Your grandmother doesn't think it's silly," Xander told him. "She thinks there's a curse on your family."

"Are you serious?" Trevor asked. "You believe that stuff?" He gave a snort that might have been laughter and shook his head, thrusting a paper at a man walking past. The man took it without looking at it or stopping. "My dad used to tell us that story when we went camping. It was scary when I was five, but I haven't believed it for a long time."

"Why didn't your grandparents say anything to us about the Beast?" Xander asked.

"Nobody here wants outsiders to know what's been going on," Trevor explained. "They think it will scare tourists away."

Xena looked at Trevor curiously. Something in his tone interested her. "But you don't think so, do you?"

"Hope not!" Trevor said with a laugh. A woman pushing a stroller crossed to their side of the street, and he handed her something.

"What are you giving them?" Xander asked.

Trevor passed him a flyer. In large bright red print it read: TREVOR'S EXCLUSIVE TOURS OF THE DEADLY BEAST OF BLACKSLOPE. £5 PER PERSON. Below the words was a crude drawing of a hairy animal with long fangs, shaggy arms outstretched.

"You're giving tours?" Xena was impressed. Five pounds was a good price, about ten dollars.

"Those two are my first clients." He jerked his head at the young couple. He reached out his hand, and Xander gave him back his flyer. "Thanks. It took forever to print these out on that ancient computer of my grandparents'. I don't want to waste any."

"So have you actually *seen* the Beast?" Xander asked. Something about Trevor's tone made him skeptical.

"I wish! No, but I take people around to places where it's been sighted, that kind of thing. The first tour leaves in a few minutes. I wanted to wait until as late as I could. Nobody's supposed to be out after sunset, but it's sort of spooky in the afternoon. Want to come along?" He smiled at them. "Since you're guests at the B and B, no charge."

"Sure!" Xena said, but Xander said, "We can't. We told our parents we'd be back soon."

"Oh, come *on*, Xander."

Xander studied his sister. Xena was so eager, and there couldn't be any harm if they went in a big group, could there?

"Well, maybe the first part." He forced the words out.

"Great," Trevor said. He turned to the couple. "Ready?"

It would have been fun even if they hadn't been on the trail of the Beast. Trevor knew a lot about the area, and he showed them tiny frogs and brightly colored birds that they never would have noticed on their own. He identified plants and told his clients what their blossoms looked like in the spring. Xander was so interested in the natural history that he'd almost forgotten about the wild animal they were hunting when the young woman asked, "So when did this Beast first appear?"

"About a century ago." Trevor's voice suddenly grew serious. "It terrorized the country-side for months." Xena noticed that the couple had drawn closer together, and the man took the woman's hand. Xena shivered. Was it the coolness of the shadowy forest or something else that suddenly raised goose bumps on her arms?

"Nobody ever found out what it was," Trevor went on, "although lots of people tried, even the famous detective Sherlock Holmes."

Xena and Xander shared a secret smile.

"But even though he later solved the case of

the mysterious Hound of the Baskervilles, he couldn't figure out what the Beast of Blackslope was. And now it's back."

Then Trevor stopped short and crouched over. "Look—footprints!" Everybody crowded around some dents in the ground. It was hard to tell exactly what they were though.

The couple took picture after picture, the flashes going nonstop.

Then the sun went behind a cloud and a cool wind rose up, scattering leaves and twigs. The woman glanced nervously at her husband. "Isn't it time we were leaving? I mean, we were going to have tea in that little café. . . ."

"Yes, yes," the man said hurriedly. "Thank you, Trevor. It was interesting but we have to get back to town now." They turned and plunged through the underbrush, nearly running.

Xander took a deep breath to slow his heart-beat. He didn't want Trevor to see how nervous the tale had made him, so he squatted and inspected the marks. He wasn't sure—were these really prints or just dents in the ground? They weren't anywhere near as clear as the one he and Xena had found.

"How did you manage to find these prints?" asked Xena.

"I hike a lot and I know the area pretty well, so I know where to look." Trevor shrugged. "You see a lot if you just keep your eyes open."

"Trevor knows altogether too much about that Beast," Xena said. "He 'stumbled on' those footprints awfully easily, didn't he?"

"Do you think he faked them?" Xander couldn't help feeling relieved at the thought.

"Maybe he did. I'm still not convinced there *is* a Beast."

"There was a real hound in *The Hound of the Baskervilles*," Xander reminded her. "Besides, what about the howls we heard?"

"I wonder if that was a didgeridoo," Xena said. "Remember, that Australian instrument Trevor talked about?"

"Do you think he's making the howling sounds with a horn?"

"Maybe," Xena said. "One thing is sure. Trevor knows more than he's saying. And remember how Mr. Tuttle said people around here wanted to keep quiet about the Beast?"

Xander nodded. "I was just thinking that. Trevor sure doesn't!"

"I know. And he's making money off the legend too. We've got another suspect—Trevor!"

CHAPTER 15

Xena was sitting alone at the table when Xander came down to breakfast the next morning.

"So?" she asked. They had decided that Xander should try to get some information out of Trevor the night before.

"Nothing." Xander shook his head. "Nada. Zilch. Zero."

"I wish *I'd* been the one to question him." Xena buttered her crumpet. "I could have gotten him to talk."

"Nuh-uh." Xander reached for the jam. "Trevor was working on a school project on American history and wanted to know all about the Declaration of Independence. He wouldn't talk about anything else."

"We'll just have to talk to him later. Let's go into town and see if we can find out anything more. That's been our best source of information so far."

They set off down Blackslope's main street. "What's all that noise?" Xena asked. She walked faster. The day had dawned bright and cool after an overnight rainstorm, and right after breakfast their parents had left to go sightseeing with some people they had met at the pre-auction viewing.

But now three cars were parked in the lot in front of the tourist agency, and loud voices were coming from the small crowd gathered on the sidewalk. One man in the crowd looked familiar. It was Mr. Whittaker.

They broke into a run, Xander straining to match his sister's pace. They slowed in front of the tourist agency, and Xena slipped into the crowd.

"All I'm telling you is what I saw," Mr. Whittaker was saying obstinately, as though someone had challenged him, "and what I heard."

"What exactly was that?" asked a stout woman wearing a business suit.

Mr. Whittaker turned to her and took off his hat. "Just what I told them earlier, Madam Mayor."

"Yes, Mr. Whittaker," she said patiently. "But I didn't hear what you said. I was indoors."

He sighed loudly and replaced his hat. "Late last night I was out on the manor grounds, going back to my cottage, when I heard something moving, near the stable. I didn't like the sound of it, it being dark and all, so I stopped where I was and ducked behind the old oak tree—you know the old oak tree by the stable?"

"Yes, yes," the mayor said. "Do go on."

"Well, as I was hiding there I saw something." He paused and looked around. Everyone, including Xander standing on the edge of the crowd, pressed in a little closer. It seemed as if all the people were holding their breath.

"And what did you see?" asked a man.

"I saw," Mr. Whittaker said, and paused again as the mayor rolled her eyes, "I saw the Beast."

A few gasps rose from the crowd.

"Go on, please, Whittaker. How did you know it was . . ." The mayor looked around. She didn't seem to notice Xena standing almost right next to her, but she lowered her voice anyway. "How did you know it was the Beast?"

"How did I *know*?" The old man sounded incredulous. "What else could it be? It was large, Madam Mayor, taller than the tallest man here, and broad. It was shaggy and the way it walked wasn't human."

Xander felt a chill creep up his spine. Mr. Whittaker sure sounded convincing.

"What did you do?" asked a woman.

"Watched it. Watched it as it climbed over a fence. You can see it now, all broken where the creature's great weight smashed it. And then off it went through the forest, knocking down shrubs and breaking branches. Then it howled, that howl we've all heard at one time or another." People nodded and murmured.

"Then what?" asked the mayor.

"Then I locked myself in my cottage until daylight and I came here to report it."

"Why didn't you call the police?"

"Phone was out," Mr. Whittaker answered. "Again, Madam Mayor," he added pointedly, as though this was her fault.

Xena looked at Xander, and he could tell what she was thinking: Maybe the Beast is real after all.

Before either one could say anything, a woman came out of the tourist agency and slammed the door behind her. The door opened again immediately, and a young man came running after her. "Please reconsider," he said.

"You brought me here under false pretenses!" the woman snapped. "All I wanted was to spend a pleasant week in the country and buy some antiques. You should tell people there's a wild animal running loose in the woods!"

She got into an expensive-looking car and drove off with a squeal of tires. Almost immediately the spot she had vacated was filled by a battered car that came from the direction of the manor house. A man hopped out and hurried into the tourist agency. A boy followed him out of the car. It was Ian, and he had a fresh bandage on his knee. That boy is such a klutz, Xander thought. He moved away from the crowd and went to say hello. "Was that your father?" he asked. Ian nodded.

Xena joined them. "What happened to you?" She pointed at his bandage.

"Oh, this?" Ian looked down at his knee. "Fell off my bike. That lady who just rode off came to argue with my mother this morning and nearly ran me over."

Raised voices came from inside the tourist agency. Through the plate-glass windows they could see people gesturing. The mayor made an exasperated sound and went inside. Xena let herself in the door.

"Not a journalist!" the mayor was saying. Her round face was pale. "And a TV crew?"

Ian's mother, who sat at a desk at the back of the room, was hanging up the phone. "That's what they told me. It will be on the news tonight."

"Wow," Xena couldn't help saying, and at that all the adults turned and looked at her.

Ian's mother shook her head. "This is not the sort of publicity we need."

The young man came back inside. "We are closed for business right now," he said, and ushered Xena out the door.

More people had joined the crowd outside, including Trevor, who was passing out flyers as fast as he could. The two college students from the B and B next door to theirs appeared. The one named Katy asked Xena, "What's going on?" Xena told her what Mr. Whittaker had related to the crowd.

"All that commotion must be why we haven't been able to catch a glimpse of the kite," Katy said to Emma.

"I bet you're right," Emma answered.

"Were you flying a kite?" Xander asked.

Emma opened her mouth as if to reply, but Katy quickly said, "That's right. We were, er, flying a kite and the string broke. Come on, Em, we need to go."

Why would a commotion at the manor keep them from finding their lost kite? wondered Xander.

Before he and Xena had a chance to ask,

Trevor came up, grinning. "I've given away all my flyers! Lots of the people who came here for the auction aren't scared by the Beast—they think it's an extra added attraction. Australia, here I come!"

"Young man!" called a woman from the other side of the street. "When does your next tour leave?"

As Trevor went over to talk to her, Xena pulled Xander around a corner out of the hubbub. "Are you thinking what I'm thinking?"

"I'm thinking two things," Xander answered. "One, Mr. Whittaker was pretty convincing. He saw *something* near the manor. And two, all this publicity is great for Trevor."

Xena nodded. "Right. Come on, it's time we put things together."

Xander pulled a pad and pencil out of his back pocket, and he and Xena sat down together on the grass in front of the library. She rubbed her hands together. "List time!"

Xander handed her the paper and pencil. "I'm going to check out that music store," he said. "It's just around the corner. Be right back."

He returned a few minutes later and flopped onto the ground. Xena could tell he was discouraged. "What?"

Xander dug his fingers into the grass. "A didgeridoo sounds *nothing* like a howl. It's kind of low and buzzy. They didn't have a recording, but the store clerk made the sound. Nobody could think it was a howl."

"Okay, I won't put it on the list," Xena said.

"So what's it a list of?"

"Suspects."

"Suspects of what?"

"Well, suppose I'm right and there is no Beast. Why would someone make it up? And who would do it?" She handed the page to Xander.

Suspect	Suspicious behavior	Motive
Mrs. Roberts	Dropped tray when hearing talk of Beast	Seems even jumpier than most people in town—why?
Trevor	Wants to go out at night, despite danger from Beast. Maybe he knows there isn't one. Could he be faking it? But why?	To make money to go to Australia
Mr. Whittaker	Touchy about stable—could Beast be hidden in it?	Something from family history?

Everybody at the manor	Beast has been sighted near there.	?
Mr. Tuttle (with a helper)	?	To sell more books
Burglar	Doors and windows locked. Burglar pretends to be Beast to scare people out of investigating.	Burglary (duh)

As Xander studied the list, their cell phone rang. This time Xander managed to answer it.

"Hello? . . . Oh, really? You're sure? . . . Well, thanks. And what about—oh." He reached for the notepad and scribbled something on a fresh page. "Okay. I'll tell you about it when we get home." He closed the phone.

"Who was that?" Xena asked.

"Andrew, calling from the SPFD lab in London. He said what we sent him isn't fur at all. It's not even human hair—it's some kind of synthetic."

Xena frowned. "That means someone must be wearing a costume."

"The howl is fake too," Xander told her. "The lab doesn't know exactly what it is yet. They're still working on that. It's more than one sound, and they have to separate them and analyze them one by one. So far they've figured out there are at least two . . ." He consulted his notes. "Two living sources, Andrew said, meaning animals, and at least one mechanical." Xander felt his fear dissolving. "That means that for sure, the Beast is a person."

"I knew it all along!" Xena jumped up and pumped her fist in the air.

"You did not."

"I *did*," Xena insisted.

"Oh, all right." Xander was too relieved to argue anymore. "But who is it? Maybe we can narrow down the suspect list a bit."

"We can probably eliminate Mrs. Roberts," Xena suggested. "She really looked scared when we came down into the kitchen after the Beast howled. If she knew it was a fake, then she wouldn't be frightened."

"Plus I think she totally believes that stuff about the family curse," Xander added. He was suddenly enjoying being a detective again.

"True." Xena crossed Mrs. Roberts off the suspect list. "Okay, so now that we know the Beast is a fake, we need to come up with some possible explanations for the Beast's appearance."

Xander eyed Xena's list of suspects. "Well, Trevor seemed eager to go out at night even though everybody was sure the Beast would attack after dark. But he wasn't afraid."

Xena tapped her pencil against the pad. "Does this mean Trevor knew there was nothing dangerous going on, maybe because he was somehow making the fake Beast sightings? Plus he's earning good money from the Beast's sudden reappearance—and he said he needed the money to go to Australia."

"So let's keep an eye on him," Xander said. "With him living in the same place we're staying, that shouldn't be too hard."

"Then there's Mr. Whittaker," Xena went on. "He wouldn't let us explore the stable at Blackslope Manor. Ian said he was breeding dogs—maybe they're really big and ferocious."

"The Hound of the Baskervilles turned out to be a real dog," Xander reminded her. "A humongous dog that terrorized everyone."

"Exactly. Maybe Mr. Whittaker lets his dogs out, or maybe sometimes they escape. People could mistake a big dog for a beast, especially in the dark and if they were scared. Then he would fake the other clues so that people wouldn't know it was his dogs and make him get rid of them."

"Why did he report seeing the Beast last night, then?"

"Maybe he was trying to keep people from finding out about his dogs."

"That would be weird, but possible, I guess," Xander said. "He did seem awfully protective of the stable."

They were silent. None of the other suspects made much sense, and neither Xander nor Xena could see where to go next. Then something occurred to Xander. "The sale at the manor is in four days. We're going back to London right after it."

"So we have got to find the Beast before we leave," Xena said. "Otherwise we'll fail Sherlock."

"I know." Xander's voice was troubled.

"What's wrong?"

"Well, it's great that there's no real beast out there. But there *is* a real person pretending to be the Beast and terrifying the whole town. He or she is repeating the pattern from the past. A sheep has already gone missing. Which means Mrs. Roberts is right about one thing: A person could be next!"

CHAPTER 16

The next morning was fresh and cool—a perfect day for the tour of the ruined castle the Holmes family had planned.

The castle wasn't enough to take Xena and Xander's minds completely off the case, but it helped. There were some walls left standing, so they could tell what the different rooms were with the help of signs posted on the dark gray stones. Exploring it was like climbing around a giant jungle gym. Xena scaled one of the shorter walls using her rock-climbing skills and pretended to pour boiling oil on Xander, who was pretending to be an enemy soldier besieging the castle. They had a good time, but both were itching to get back on the case.

They stopped at a restaurant in the country for supper and got back to the B and B late. As Xander was climbing into bed, Xena appeared at his door carrying two flashlights. "Take one of these. I found them on the end table in the sitting room. Nobody will mind if we borrow them. And keep your shoes next to your bed. We have to be ready to go at a moment's notice."

"What makes you think we'll be going somewhere tonight?" Xander quickly switched the flashlight on and off again, then put it under his pillow.

"I don't know," Xena admitted, "but we have to be ready for anything."

"All I'm ready for," Xander mumbled into his pillow, "is sleep." Xena could be so bossy. He knew she was right, though, and tried to stay awake. But all that climbing in the fresh air had exhausted them, and first Xander and then Xena fell asleep.

But not for long. A howl rose through the night, reaching a pitch so high it sounded like a woman's scream, and then sinking to a long, low sob that lingered in the air.

Xena and Xander met at the front door of the B and B, each clutching a flashlight.

"Which way did it come from?" Xander asked. His heart was pounding. It's not really the Beast, he tried to tell himself.

"That way!" Xena gestured with her flashlight and clicked the On button. Finally a chance to get a sighting of the Beast! But no light appeared. "Darn!" she said, and took off running. She wasn't going to let it get away. "Turn yours on, Xander!" she called behind her.

"I'm trying!" he said, trotting after her while pressing the button. Weak yellow light came out the front of the flashlight but faded seconds later.

"I don't believe this!" Xander said. "It worked when I turned it on before." He shook the flashlight and tried again. No luck.

Xena turned back. There was no point—the darkness was as thick as a wall. Unless the Beast was standing in the middle of the road waving its arms, they'd never see it. She stopped and waited for her brother to catch up with her.

"Xander, stop messing with the flashlight. The battery's dead."

He looked up. "How do you know?" He smacked the flashlight against the palm of his hand.

She took it from him. "You'll just break the bulb. There's no point."

Xander followed her back to the B and B. He was secretly relieved that their mission had to be postponed until daylight. Even if the Beast was a person in a costume, he wasn't eager to meet that person in the middle of the night.

Xena, though, was genuinely disappointed. "The way Mr. Whittaker described the Beast, it didn't move very fast. I bet I could have caught up with it if I was able to see where I was going."

"I always thought it was just a saying that your hair stands up on your head when you're scared." Xander rubbed his hand over the back of his neck, which still felt tingly. "But it really happens!"

"I was a little spooked too," Xena admitted. "I wonder if Mom and Dad heard the howl."

"I don't think so. They're on the other side of the house. And they'd probably be out here by now if they had."

The only light on was the one left burning all night to light the way to the bathroom. The sitting room, the kitchen, everything else was dark. Xena and Xander tiptoed up the stairs, and as they passed Trevor's room Xander noticed that his door was ajar. It had always been shut tight before, so this was odd. Xander pushed the door with his fingertips, and it moved a little. He gave it a good shove and it swung all the way open.

The light from the hall was weak but their eyes were accustomed to the darkness by now, and they could see that Trevor's bed was empty.

"Strange," Xena mused. "Where could he be in the middle of the night?"

"Bathroom?"

Xena looked down the hall and shook her head. "Door's open and nobody's in there."

"Maybe he went outside to see what the howling was."

"Maybe," Xena said, "and maybe not. He could be the one out there howling and making footprints!" They locked eyes, a combination of certainty and excitement growing inside them.

"Let's try to catch him when he comes back," Xander said. "We'll have to stake out his room."

Xander took the first watch. "If I hide in the linen closet with the door cracked, I'll be able to see if anyone goes in or out without being seen."

"Just don't fall asleep in there," Xena cautioned. "I'll come in a few hours."

Xander made himself a kind of nest out of pillows and blankets. He sat bolt upright and stared at Trevor's door until he thought his eyes had dried out. He blinked and rubbed them, fighting the urge to sleep.

Why was it that time went so fast when you were having fun and so slowly when you weren't? The sounds of the house around him were cozy as little clicks and creaks reached him every once in a while. He heard the sitting-room clock strike the hour, then again, and again. Surely Xena would come for him soon.

He didn't realize he had fallen asleep until another sound woke him. He sat up, feeling the insides of his ears tickle. It wasn't a howl, and it wasn't footsteps. It was a regular and high-pitched *beep-beep-beep*. What could it be?

Then he recognized it—Xena's alarm clock. She must have set it before she went back to bed so that she could relieve him on time. Good. He stood and stretched, aching for his bed.

Why wasn't Xena turning off the alarm? And why wasn't she relieving him? If she didn't shut off the alarm soon, it was liable to wake one of the adults. Then a worse thought came to him— what if something had happened to her? What if whoever was pretending to be the Beast had gone into Xena's room and snatched her away? Xander jumped to his feet in a sudden panic. Wait a minute, he told himself. He took a few deep breaths. Why would it come for Xena? He had to be logical about this. Then Xander's fear level shot back up as another question occurred to him: What about Trevor? After all, his grandmother had said the Beast might come for him!

Cautiously, Xander pushed open the linen-closet door. No light, no sound aside from that annoying beep, no motion. He forced himself not to run but to take long silent steps as he moved toward the bedrooms. He reached Trevor's door and glanced in. Still nobody.

He let himself into Xena's room. For a moment he couldn't tell if the bundle on the bed was a pile of bunched-up sheets or his sister's sleeping form, but then he heard a light snore and a grunt.

Phew. It was Xena. He turned off the alarm and shook her shoulder.

She rolled over. "Leave me alone," she muttered into her pillow. "'S not time to get up yet. 'S still dark."

"Xena!" He shook her again. "I'm not Mom! I'm Xander, and you were supposed to take over the watch." He yawned hugely. "Get up!"

Xena sat up, her hair messy, her eyes half-open. She glanced at the window. The sky was a light charcoal gray. "Look, it's getting light," she said. "Did Trevor come back?"

"Nope. Let's go look for him!" Maybe now that the sun was rising they would be able to see something.

Xander got their sweaters while Xena

dressed, and then they went out together. Birds were twittering in the trees, and the dawn air was cool.

"Look!" Xander said. "We're in luck!" He pointed at the dew that lay on the grass. Someone—or something—had walked over it, leaving a clear trail.

"It will burn away as soon as the sun's really out," Xena said. "Come on!"

They took off running. The trail led through the garden and down a slope. They had to climb over fences and let themselves through gates, and once Xander nearly ran into a drowsy sheep. Every time the trail faded they took their best guess as to where it would lead; every time they managed to pick it up again.

When they paused to catch their breath Xena said, "You know, you can tell where it's going."

Xander nodded. "Straight into the woods."

"Right. And this means . . . ?"

He knew what she was getting at. "It means we have to go into the woods after it." Even if the Beast wasn't really a beast, even if it was a human, there was something weird going on. And who knew what other animals might be lurking in the shadows? Nocturnal animals with sharp eyes that could see him when he couldn't see them. He shivered and glanced behind him. Nothing.

"Xander." Xena's voice was quiet. "I have to tell you something."

"What?"

She looked him right in the eye. "I know this case scares you, but you've never backed off. I think you're really brave. And we'll keep together the whole time, okay?"

"Okay." Xander took a deep breath, tried to smile, and ran off with his sister. Soon they were surrounded by trees. They paused, wondering where to go next.

"There isn't anything here," Xander said. It didn't *look* like there were any wild animals nearby, but still—

"Wait!" Xena grabbed her brother's arm. "What's that?"

Xander strained to hear, and thought he caught the sound of rustling leaves and cracking branches behind them.

Then an unmistakable sound reached their ears. It was a howl, and as it rose and quavered in the air they realized it was close. Very close.

"Climb a tree!" Xander said. "The Beast is right on top of us!"

But before Xena could move, a voice came from somewhere in front of them. "I *thought* there was someone following me! What are you two doing out here?"

It was Trevor.

But Xena had a different question. "If you were in front of us, what made the noise?" She pointed to her left.

For a second all three looked at one another, and then they said simultaneously, "The Beast!"

Xena said, "Come on! It's getting away!" and they took off. They couldn't run fast, since they had to push their way through branches and climb over fallen logs.

Xander fell into step beside Trevor. "So what were you doing out here?" Xander asked. "Why did you sneak out? Weren't you afraid your grandmother would think the Beast got you?"

"She and my grandfather sleep till seven," Trevor said, panting as they hurried after Xena. "I'll be back before then. And I'm doing the same thing I bet you're doing—tracking the Beast."

"Come on!" Xena called. She had pulled way ahead. "There's a path over here."

The two boys pushed their way through the underbrush. Xena was already running down the trail. They pounded after her but even at top speed they couldn't catch up. She rounded a turn and they lost sight of her.

It was getting lighter as the dawn spread across the sky, but Xander felt a sudden prickle of fear. In this thick forest anything seemed possible. Could they be wrong? Was there really a Beast of Blackslope? He pushed the thought away.

The path forked and the two boys slowed down. Which way had Xena gone?

Trevor held out an arm to keep Xander back, and bent down close to the dirt. He straightened. "This way!" They started running again. Xander had a stitch in his side, but he gritted his teeth and kept going.

Then, from straight in front of them, came the beginnings of another howl. Straining to see through the trees, Xander made out a bright light shining not too far away. The howl stopped abruptly. There was silence for a moment, then someone screamed and the light went out.

"Xena!" Xander called. "Where are you?"

CHAPTER 17

Xander took off running toward the light. Xena never screamed without good reason. Beast or no Beast, his rage at whatever it was that had threatened his sister overcame his fear.

"It came from over here!" Trevor called.

"No, the light was in this direction!" What if the Beast had gotten his sister? Where could they go for help in the woods? Stay calm, Xander told himself.

Trevor caught up with him. "The light could have been anything, but the scream was from that direction." He pointed left.

Xander stopped and bent over, hands on his knees, trying to catch his breath. He felt all turned around.

"Okay, you go toward the scream. I'll follow the light."

"I don't think we should split up." Trevor cast a nervous glance over his shoulder.

"Well, let's go *somewhere*." Xander's anxiety was growing.

"Xena!" they both called. "Where are you?"

Nothing. "Okay, I guess we do have to split up," Trevor admitted. "I'll go this way, and you—"

Just then they heard a whistle.

"That's her!" Xander ran toward the sound, suddenly afraid of what he would see when he got there. Would he find his sister clutched in huge shaggy paws? He let out a big breath of relief when he saw Xena sitting on a log holding her right ankle.

"I tripped," she said. Xander reached down and helped her up. She put her weight on her left leg. "If you guys had quit arguing, you would have heard me calling earlier."

Xander couldn't feel irritated at her angry tone. He was so relieved to see her safe and reasonably sound that he would have hugged her if Trevor hadn't been there.

"Is that why you screamed?" Trevor asked. "When you fell, I mean."

"That wasn't me. That was way down there." She gestured into the trees.

"Where's the Beast?" Xander looked all around.

"Lost it." Xena sounded angry at herself. "I

could hear it for a while, but it seemed to know the woods really well. By the time I found this path it had disappeared, and I have no idea which way it went."

"Can you walk?" Xander asked.

"You stay here with her," Trevor said. "I'll go see if I can pick up a trail." He sped off.

Xena got up and tested her ankle. "I'm okay. It's not sprained." She spoke with the authority of an athlete who had experienced injuries. "Let me lean on you a bit." With her hand pressing down on Xander's shoulder, they followed in Trevor's path.

They found him in a clearing where the grass had been trampled flat. Xena plopped down onto a large rock with a sigh, holding her ankle, and Xander bent over the grass looking for clues.

After a few minutes he said, "This is weird. Look!" and pointed to three holes in the dirt that formed a triangle with corners about two feet apart.

"Huh." Trevor squatted next to him and peered at the holes. "I wonder what could have made those."

Xander studied it again. He measured the distance between the holes with his hands.

"There are lots of prints here." Trevor pointed to the middle of the cleared area. Xander joined him. "These look like shoes, but those other prints were made by something else. Like a big flat foot."

"Which way do they go?" Xena called from her perch on the rock.

Trevor followed the prints across the clearing and into a thicket of trees. A few moments later he returned. "It's no use," he reported. "I can't track it. The branches of all those trees protected the path from the rain. The ground is dry and there aren't any clear prints. Come on, let's go home."

Xena and Xander had had enough for one night, so they agreed and headed back to the B and B, Xena limping on her twisted ankle. It was full daylight by the time they got back. Trevor stopped them at the door. "Don't tell my grandparents. I don't want to worry them."

You mean you don't want to get grounded again, Xena thought, but all she said was, "All right."

"You can count on us," Xander promised.

They slept most of the morning, and when they got up they found a note on Xander's door. "See you later, sleepyheads!" it said in their mother's handwriting. "We've gone exploring. Money for lunch on my bureau. Be back before tea time."

"Let's go to town," Xander said. "I'm starving."

Xena's ankle hadn't swelled up, and if she walked carefully it didn't hurt. They made their way slowly to a café and ordered sandwiches. They were finishing their lunch when Katy and Emma, the university students from next door, stopped at their table.

"Hullo, you two!" said Emma. "What have you been up to?"

"Not much," Xander said. "Exploring."

Katy leaned forward and plucked something out of his hair. "Exploring in the woods?" She showed him a twig she had pulled out of the blond streak in his dark curls.

"Yup," he agreed, and then he pulled a tiny leaf off the sleeve of her sweater. "You too?"

For a second she looked like she was about to deny it, but then she laughed. "You have sharp eyes! That leaf matches my sweater exactly."

"So what were you doing out there?" Xena asked quickly, before the girls got a chance to ask them first.

Katy and Emma looked at each other as though unwilling to explain. "Oh, come on,"

Xander said with his winning smile. As people usually did, Katy and Emma melted.

"We're making a film," Emma said. "A documentary about a bird called the red kite."

"The kite!" Xena exclaimed. "I *knew* you weren't talking about one of those things on a string!"

"Sorry we told you a story," Katy said. "A kite's a kind of bird. It's rare and very shy, and we heard one had been sighted near here. So we decided to film it for our final class project. But there's always noise in the forest at dusk, which is normally when we'd have the best chance of seeing it. It seems to have been scared off by something."

"Aha!" Xena said. The others looked at her. "That's why you told us to search on the other side of the town!"

. "Yes," Emma said. "The more people in the forest, the less chance we have of finding it."

"Oh!" Xander said. "So that was film equipment you were carrying when we saw you that first time!" The waitress brought the trifle he had ordered, but he was so intrigued by what the girls were saying that the layers of cake, custard, and jam didn't even tempt him.

The girls nodded. "We had to be secretive

about it," Katy said. "We keep it in the shed so that the others won't see what we have."

"What others?" Xander asked.

"There's a prize for the best film, and another of the crews from our school is working nearby," Emma explained. "We didn't want them to know we were here."

"What kind of equipment do you use?" Xena asked.

"Oh, cameras and lights and tripods," Katy answered. "And filters for the lenses, and all sorts of things."

"Anything with brown fuzzy material on it?" The girls looked at her questioningly, and Xena flushed. She knew it was an odd question. "Like insulation or padding or something?"

"No," Emma answered, still looking curious.

Before her friend could say anything else, Katy said, "But now that we know about the Beast, there's no way we'll be going into those woods again!"

"We have to," Emma said. "It's too late to start another film."

"How do you go about looking for the kite?" Xena asked.

"Oh, we know where it likes to hang out," Katy said. "And we have a recording of its call."

Xander pricked up his ears. "Could we hear the recording?"

Emma shrugged. "I don't see why not." Out of her backpack she pulled a portable CD player. "Put these on." She gave Xander the headphones. He sat up straighter. Was he about to hear the howl? Emma pressed the Start button, and Xena pulled one of the earpieces away from her brother's head so that she could hear too.

For a second, nothing. Then—

"*Scrawk!*" The shrill scream wasn't very pleasant but was unmistakably a birdcall, and nothing like the heart-stopping howls that had been ringing out at dusk and in the night.

"Thanks." Xander pulled off the headphones and handed them back to her. "Very interesting." He picked up a spoon and dug into his trifle. He was so disappointed, he hardly tasted it.

"Yeah, thanks," echoed Xena.

Emma wound the cord around the headphones and tucked them into her backpack. "Everyone's been really nice and helpful. But I don't know. We might just have to take an incomplete for this assignment." She started walking away down the sidewalk.

"Come on, now, Emma," Katy said. "Let's talk this over." She took off after her friend.

"How big do you think those camera tripods are?" Xander asked his sister.

Xena shrugged. "I don't know, but the cameras must be pretty heavy. Why?"

"You know those holes in the woods?" Xena nodded. "Do you think they were made by something like that?"

"Hmm . . ." She frowned in concentration. "Could be. We should have asked Katy and Emma if they've been out that way."

"Going to make a list of questions we need to ask?"

Xena ignored his teasing. "It's time we got some answers." She fished in her pocket for the money to pay for their lunch. "Eat up and let's go find Trevor."

At first Trevor didn't want to tell Xena and Xander anything.

"Come on," Xander said. "We already know a lot about what's going on. We're pretty sure this isn't a real beast, just someone dressed up in a costume."

"Do you have any proof?" Trevor asked.

"No," Xena admitted. "But we'll keep looking. Everybody slips up sometime. And it's obviously someone who knows the woods well, like you."

Trevor looked like he was about to say something, but he closed his mouth.

"And the manor house has something to do with it," Xena went on. "A lot of the sightings came from near there. So maybe the Beast hides out there or something."

Trevor still didn't say anything. "Come on," Xander said. "Your grandparents are awake half the night worrying, and lots of people are starting to panic. If this keeps up, *all* the tourists will stop coming, not just the ones who get scared easily, and your guide business will flop."

Trevor looked from one to the other, and then seemed to make up his mind. "Okay," he said. "It's like this. I've been tracking the Beast's movements. I've always wanted to be a naturalist, and I knew that if I was the first to find the Beast, I'd get my name known right away. Maybe I'd even have my own TV show. So I've been keeping track of all the places where the Beast has been sighted. And I've found some things—"

"What things?" Xander burst in.

"Come on," Trevor said. "I'll show you."

They followed him out to a different part of the woods from where they'd been at dawn. On the way he pointed out clues to them: footprints, broken branches, crushed leaves.

"Aha!" Xander snatched something off the ground. He held up the wrapper of a protein bar, triumphant.

"I don't think a beast would eat one of those," Trevor said.

"No way," Xena said. "Chickens and things, sure. Maybe even a human once in a while. But not peanut butter–cranberry protein bars!"

"Maybe chicken-flavored protein bars!" Trevor said with a laugh.

"Maybe human-flavored—" But Xander didn't get to finish his sentence, because suddenly they heard, off in the distance, the sound of the birdcall that Katy and Emma had played for them the day before. They stopped in their tracks.

"What was that?" Trevor asked.

"A birdcall," Xena said. "Those girls from the other B and B are making a movie."

Trevor didn't move. "I wonder," he said thoughtfully. "You know, those girls arrived before you, and the day they came was when the Beast sightings started. Maybe that was just a coincidence, but maybe they have something to do with it. We should see what they're up to."

"Let's go now," Xander suggested.

Trevor glanced at his watch and grimaced. "I can't," he said. "I've got to get back. I promised my grandmother I'd help her clean out her shed today."

"Can't you do that some other time?" Xander asked.

Trevor shook his head. "No, it wouldn't be fair to Gran. I've already put it off twice." His face suddenly brightened. "The shed! I completely forgot to tell you. We have a couple of bikes in the shed. You could borrow them if you want and take them to look for the film crew. It'll be faster than going on foot."

They walked back with Trevor as fast as Xena's sore ankle would allow them. While Xander ran inside to ask Mrs. Roberts to tell their parents they'd gone for a bike ride, Trevor set Xena up with the two bicycles and helmets.

The road was flat and smooth and the day was beautiful. Xander joined her and they wheeled the bikes out.

"Your ankle okay?" Xander asked.

Xena nodded. "It's just a twist. I've done a lot worse in a soccer game and still scored a goal!"

Xander threw one leg over the smaller bike and pushed off. "Isn't this great?" But there was no answer. He turned and saw Xena sitting on the bike seat, one foot on a pedal, the other on the ground. Her mouth was hanging open.

"What is it?"

Xena didn't answer him for a second, but then she turned shining eyes on him. "Xander! I think I know who's pretending to be the Beast— and why!"

"What do you mean? Who is it?"

"Remember how Trevor told us all this started when the college students arrived?" Xena said as she put on her helmet. They started to ride a little way down the street. "They use lights when they make movies, right? That birdcall came from a different part of the forest than the light. So the light must have come from one of the other groups from their school. Why would someone come out here to this little town for a film project? Only if there's something here they can't find anyplace else."

"Like that kite," Xander said. He thought he could see where Xena's thoughts were heading, and he started pumping the pedals faster as his heart sped.

"Right. Or the Beast of Blackslope!"

They came to a red light, and a young woman on a motor scooter wearing a hot pink helmet was waiting for the cross traffic to stop. She was talking on a cell phone as her scooter pumped smelly dark gray smoke into the air.

Xena didn't want to keep talking about their investigation in front of a stranger, and anyway, she could never resist eavesdropping. Besides, if someone has a conversation right out in the open, it isn't really private, she reasoned. She leaned in a little closer, trying not to breathe in deeply because of the fumes.

This time she heard even more than she was hoping for. The woman was saying, "But what am I supposed to do? Don't you think I should run and scream? It's scary enough with those fangs and that ratty-looking fur. I don't understand why—" At that moment the light turned green and she gunned her engine, the noisy scooter drowning out the rest of her words as she sped through the intersection.

Xena and Xander took one look at each other. "The Beast!" Xena said, and she took off, Xander pedaling madly to keep up with her.

Luckily the road went slightly downhill as it left the town, and they were able to keep the motor scooter in sight. Even when it rounded a curve they could keep on the trail as its noisy engine announced its location.

They were gaining on the woman when she turned down a country lane. Xander stood on his pedals for a burst of speed and managed to pass

Xena, who was slowed by her ankle. They were close enough that if the scooter hadn't been so noisy, they could have called out and asked her to stop. But before they could do so, a flock of sheep suddenly appeared, bumping into one another and baaing and making a commotion.

"Quick! Let's go across the field!" said Xander, puffing.

"No use." Xena stopped and balanced herself with her good foot. "It's too bumpy and uneven. We'd have to walk the bikes around the rest of the flock and then wheel them over the field. It will be quicker to wait. The sheep can't cross the road forever."

But it *seemed* like forever before the last few stragglers were hurrying across the lane to catch up to the others, bleating pitifully as though to say "Wait for me!"

"Go!" said Xena, and she pushed off, Xander close behind.

They arrived at a fork in the road and paused. Xena cocked her head and listened: nothing. No beastly howling, no racket of the motor scooter's engine. "Where could she be?" she asked in frustration. Xander hopped off his bike and bent over, looking down.

"What's the point?" Xena asked irritably.

"There are so many tracks here, how could you figure out which one is the scooter's?"

"Look!" He pointed at the road. "A drop of oil! Remember how much smoke her scooter was making? I bet there's an oil leak, like when our car had one and Dad called it Old Smoky!"

"I bet you're right!" Xena said. "Let's go!"

They took off down the left-hand fork. But this time they didn't have to go far.

Leaning against the hedge at the side of the road was the scooter. The woman's hot pink helmet lay on the ground next to it. Xander jumped off his bike and ran to the scooter. "What could have happened to her?" he asked.

At that moment the underbrush shook, and something stepped out. But it wasn't the motor-scooter woman. It was a huge, hairy beast, and it was growling. Xena and Xander cried out and clung together as it lifted its massive clawed paws above them.

CHAPTER 18

Cut!" someone cried from the bushes.

The Beast stopped in its tracks and lowered its arms. In the daylight it was easy to see it was a person wearing a costume. Torn patches of the shaggy light brown fur were roughly mended, and the eyes were blank glass. The shoulders were obviously padded, giving it an ape-like appearance. Vicious fangs stuck out of its mouth. Rubbery-looking paw pads ended in long plastic claws. A strange sound came from the head of the Beast— could it be a muffled laugh?

"It's just a movie." Xena's voice wobbled. She couldn't tell if she was about to laugh too, or if she was on the verge of tears. Even though she'd figured it couldn't be real, when the Beast jumped out at them it seemed completely believable.

"Why did you yell cut? Did I miss my cue?" came a voice from the bushes, and out stepped the woman who'd been riding the scooter. Only now, instead of jeans and a denim jacket, she was wearing a long filmy gown and high heels. She wobbled on the uneven ground, and a red-headed young man who had also just emerged from the underbrush grabbed her arm.

"Steady, there!" he said with a laugh. "Can't have Lady What's-her-name break an ankle!"

"What's going on?" Xander asked, but Xena said, "I bet I know!"

The couple turned to her. "What do you know?" asked the man.

"You're making a movie, aren't you?"

"Yes," said the man. "We're calling it *Death on the Downs*. Good title, don't you think?"

A third person hurried up to them. She looked about the same age as the others, college students like Katy and Emma. She was smiling at Xena and Xander. "That was great! You two looked terrified. Marvelous! I'd like to keep that shot in the film. I'm Susan, the director."

"We weren't *really* scared," Xander said.

"No, just startled," Xena confirmed. "We already figured out that the Beast was a person in a costume."

"Still, it's one thing to know and yet another to have it pop out of the bushes at you, isn't it?" Susan said with a grin.

"Are we taking a break?" asked a muffled voice from inside the Beast. "Because if we are, I want to get out of this thing. It's hot in here."

The scooter woman undid some snaps around its neck and pulled the head off. Then she unzipped the back of the costume and pulled down the shoulders, revealing a blond young man whose hair was plastered with sweat. He must have been looking through holes in the chest of the Beast, since its head was well above his own.

"Phew!" he said. "That's better."

"We're making one of those mockumentaries," the redheaded man explained. "You know, it will look like it was filmed by a news crew as it happened, but really it's a regular film, with a script and actors and everything."

"I play Lady Periwinkle," said the woman who had been riding the motor scooter. "It's the starring role!"

"No, the Beast is really the star," teased the blond man.

"You've got to be joking," said the woman. "You don't even use your own voice for the howl!"

"What is that sound anyway?" Xena asked.

The redheaded man seemed eager to explain. "I made it out of a mixture of effects. There's a bloodhound and a peacock—"

"A peacock?" Xander asked.

"Yes, that's the screech. And a train whistle and a beluga whale. I mixed them all. I'm the technician."

"So you're the one in charge of lights and things?" Xena asked. He nodded.

Xander walked over to one of the tall spotlights. With his hands he measured the distance between its legs. "I was right! It was the tripod that made those holes!"

"We saw one of your lights this morning around dawn," Xena said to the red-haired man. "It was really bright."

"It has to be when we're filming in dim light," he explained. "Otherwise you lose a lot of detail. We use a filter to keep it from looking like the middle of the day."

"But the other nights when we heard the howl, I didn't see any light," Xander said. "And it's so bright that we would have seen one."

"Early this morning was our first time filming in the dark. It's hard enough getting around in this costume without stumbling over things."

"You mean like the post near the rosebushes in the village?" Xena asked.

The blond man groaned. "Yes. The first time I tried on the costume was our first night in the

148

village. I lifted my arm and one of my fingertips got stuck on the wooden slats! The costume's arms are at least a foot longer than my own, and they're hard to control. I had to tug at it until the end ripped off. How on earth did you know about that?"

"We found some fur," Xena said.

"And you took the newspapers from the library to get details about the Beast sightings a hundred years ago, right?" Xander added, eager to confirm all the details.

"Newspapers? I didn't take any newspapers." The technician looked puzzled. "Did you, Susan?"

The director shook her head. "Not me. I finished my share of the research before we came."

"Derek?" The man in the Beast costume shook his head, and for good measure shook the Beast's head in his hand too.

"Maggie?" But the woman playing Lady Periwinkle denied it too. Understandable, Xena thought. Nobody wants to confess to it in front of us. It's pretty sneaky, taking something from a public library.

"So why've you been making all that noise at night?" Xander crossed his fingers, hoping they'd slip up and admit they'd been out late.

"We haven't been," said the director. "I told you, early this morning was our first time out in the dark."

"But wait a second," Xena said. "If it wasn't you, who was it?"

"Maybe there is a Beast after all," Xander said. He tried to sound like he was joking but his nervousness must have come through, because the others fell quiet.

Xena broke the silence. "I bet someone's using your costume!"

Susan considered this. "That other team, maybe. The ones doing that bird film." Her voice was scornful. "They're so competitive—they'll do anything to get their film done first. Maybe they're stealing the costume at night. Remember that morning when we found some rips in it?" she asked one of her crew.

"But why would they?" one of the other students objected. "And how? Our props are locked up in the shed every night. Nobody in the crew would tell anyone the combination to the lock."

"Hmm." Xander thought about this. The film would account for some Beast sightings, maybe, but there was no reason for the students to lie about whether or not they'd been making the noises at night. Someone else must have been doing that.

"Where's this shed?" Xena asked.

"On the estate," Susan said. "Blackslope Manor. On the end of the stable where the old man keeps his dogs."

Xander drew Xena aside. "I bet that's not a shed!" He was practically dancing up and down with excitement. "I bet it's the apartment that Adeline the cook lived in with her husband!"

CHAPTER 19

Back to work," the director said. "Places, everybody! And you two—seriously, I'd like to use that shot in the picture. Do you think your parents would sign a permission form?"

"Sure," Xander said, and he told her where they were staying.

"And there's one more thing," Susan said. "Our film is in a competition with the other team that's shooting here in Blackslope. We've been telling everyone we're filming a nature documentary. No one knows what we're really doing, and we're trying to keep it all very hush-hush."

"No problem," Xena said. "We won't tell."

The Beast put his head back on, and soon all the actors were running around and screaming and getting caught. Xander and Xena turned to go. Normally they would have loved to stay and watch, but they were burning to get over to the manor and check out the stable.

"Race you!" Xander said.

"No fair!" Xena said. "I'm injured."

So they rode their bikes at a steady pace. Soon the wide sweeping drive of the estate opened in front of them, and they turned into it. "I hope nobody comes and tells us to get out of here," said Xander, feeling naked in front of all those huge windows.

"That's a chance we have to take," said Xena.

As they neared the house they saw someone leaning a sign against a post in the drive. Xander slowed down. "It's Ian!"

Ian turned around. When he saw who it was, he raised a hand in greeting. "What are you doing here?" he asked.

"Oh—well—" Xander couldn't think of anything to say, but Xena leaped in.

"We borrowed these bikes and couldn't think of anyplace to ride to, so we thought we'd come out here and see you. What are you doing?"

Ian stood back and let them see the sign. SALE CANCELED, it said.

"The auction's been canceled?" Xena asked. "But why?"

"Lots of people who were going to bid on things left because of the Beast."

"Wow, sorry," Xander said. "Your family must be really disappointed."

"Yeah, sorry," Xena said.

"They're still selling the house though." Ian kicked at the gravel. "They say that some rich person from another country probably won't have heard about the Beast, or they won't care."

"I guess since you don't really live here you won't be too upset about that," Xander said.

"I do so live here," Ian said. "I lived here year-round when I was little, and I've spent every summer and most holidays here ever since I went to school."

Xena and Xander felt awkward, but they didn't know Ian well enough to know what to say. He seemed uncomfortable too and after a few moments he said, "Well, I have to go. Feel free to look around." He raised a hand to them again and turned back to the house. He tripped over the step but kept his footing this time.

"Let's go look at the shed or apartment or whatever it is," Xena said. They walked their bikes around to the other side of the house. There was the stable, and there too was Mr. Whittaker, sitting on a wooden bench and smoking a pipe. He didn't look angry this time—he looked sad.

They propped their bikes against the wall of the stable and sat down next to him. He seemed surprised to see them.

"We're sorry about the sale," Xander said in a soft voice.

"Thanks, son," Mr. Whittaker said. "I won't deny that it's breaking my heart, the idea of leaving my old home. I thought I'd live out my days in my cottage back there and be buried in the family graveyard when my time came. It's easy for young people. They don't have the ties to the place that we old folks have."

"Sorry," Xena said. "Will you be able to raise your dogs in your new place?"

This turned out to be the right thing to say. The old man's face lit up. "Aye, that's one blessing. There's a nice little garden and I can put up a fence."

"A little garden?" Xena was surprised. "Don't your dogs need lots of room?"

"Oh, no, just a brisk walk every day and a bit of a garden to run in," Mr. Whittaker said. "Here, come and see for yourselves."

He must have decided that we're not dog spies, Xena thought as they followed the old man around to the front of the stable. Mr. Whittaker pulled open the heavy door, and out bounded three small silky brown and white dogs with long ears and furiously wagging tails. Xena squatted down and held out her arms, and one of the dogs pranced up to her, put its paws on her knees, and licked her face frantically.

"What are they?" she asked between dog kisses. "They're so cute!"

"Cavalier King Charles spaniels," the old man said proudly. "Champion bloodline. That one there is Blackslope's Bonny Sultana. I call her Bonny. Haven't you seen Cavs before?"

"No, I don't think we have many of them in the States." Xander picked up a wriggling dog.

"That one's Chimington's Dandy Darling," said Mr. Whittaker. "Her pups are almost ready to find new homes. Come see them." He walked ahead of them, leaning heavily on his cane.

"He's like a grandpa with his new grandchildren," Xena whispered as they followed him into the stable.

They blinked to accustom their eyes to the dim light. The sweet scent of straw mixed with the pleasant smell of well-kept horses. The speckled white face of a small pony looked out curiously at them from one stall, and in the next a large brown horse munched on something, its long tail swishing.

Mr. Whittaker was leaning over a wooden pen. "She can't have gotten out," he muttered, his forehead creased in a worried frown.

"Are you missing one?" Xander asked. Two puppies were dancing all over each other in the pen, their big brown eyes sparkling, their tails wagging in a blur.

"A little female," he said. "Tricolor. Where can she be? They're not big enough to climb out of their pen."

"We'll help you look," Xena said. They pawed through clumps of straw and lifted the black and red blanket to peer under it. After a minute Xena noticed that Xander was no longer helping in the search.

"What, did you give up already?" she asked him, and then looked closer. With his finger Xander was tracing a pattern in the dust of the stable floor.

"Xena," he said, "look at this." He had drawn a rectangle with a little square on the end.

"I don't get it."

"Don't you remember?" Xander asked. "From the notebook?" Xena shook her head impatiently. Sometimes Xander seemed to think everybody had his photographic memory. "Sherlock drew the manor house," he explained.

"This is the stable, and it looks like there's a door at the end of it. And if Sherlock didn't turn the drawing around"—he stood and pointed to the wall that blocked off the puppy pen—"the door is over here."

They pulled aside the heavy bales of hay as Mr. Whittaker watched, leaning on his cane.

Sure enough, there was a door. And the gap between its bottom and the floor of the stable was big enough to allow a puppy to wriggle under it, as Xander discovered when he pulled the door open and a little black, brown, and white puppy came hurtling out to join its mother and siblings.

"Well, I'll be!" Mr. Whittaker said. "I'd forgotten about that door. It goes to the room where the coachman and cook used to live, early in the last century. My old dad used it as a shed and so do I, but we've always gone into it from the outside."

Xena and Xander walked away to confer.

"Did you see anything in there?" Xena asked.

"There was a lot of gardening stuff piled against the door. And there was a big boom box. I bet that's the one they use for howls. There was a lot of junk too, like piles of old paper and a garden hose and some tools. But there was also other stuff that looked like it could be used in a movie."

"So now we know that the Beast costume is probably stored in there and also that somebody could have gotten into the shed, even with the door locked. All they'd have to do is come through the stable."

"That's not so easy," objected Xander. "Remember how ferocious Mr. Whittaker was when we came here the first time? He wouldn't even let us touch the stable door. Maybe someone could sneak past him once or twice, but I bet he'd catch them sooner or later."

"True." Xena thought a moment. "So it must be a person he trusts or someone he's so used to seeing around that he wouldn't notice them coming and going at different times."

"Ian!" breathed Xander.

CHAPTER 20

I t's got to be Ian," Xander went on. "He said he's
spent a lot of time here, every summer and lots
of holidays. Any kid exploring in the stable
would have found that door. If the costume and
the boom box are in there, he'd have no trouble
taking them.

"And," he added as a thought struck him,
"remember that first time we saw him? Remember
how he kept sneezing? Maybe he'd been reading
those old newspapers! They made my nose run in
the library, and I forgot to wash my hands so all the
mold and dust and stuff made me sneeze later too.
What if Ian was researching the Beast?"

"But why would he pretend to be the Beast?"

"Lots of reasons. He's bored, right? He keeps
saying how dull it is here. What could be more
exciting than scaring people with this Beast
thing? Plus maybe he doesn't really want the old
family stuff to get sold. Remember how happy we

160

were when they gave us Sherlock's cold-case book back in London? What if someone tried to sell it? Wouldn't you do something to stop them?"

"I sure would," Xena agreed. "And we've got to do something now. Let's set up another stake-out. We have to see who's going into and out of that stable."

Xander called the B and B on his cell phone. Their parents were still away so he asked Mr. Roberts to tell them that he and Xena were spending the night at the manor. He didn't exactly say that Ian had invited them to sleep over, and he also didn't mention that they'd be outside after dark watching a stable.

Xena and Xander found a comfortable spot behind a thick bush where they could observe the shed and the stable door without being seen.

As dark fell, it got cooler. The slender moon of just a few days ago was gone, and the stars twinkled coldly in the black sky. They had gotten used to all the lights of London, even at night. The country was so dark. An owl hooted in the distance and once in a while they could hear something small scurrying near them.

"I wish we'd brought a blanket, or a couple of sweaters," Xander said, more to break the silence than anything else. His voice sounded too loud.

Xena grunted in agreement. Xander went on: "Remember when Ian tripped and hurt his leg and it made him limp?" Xena nodded. "Now that I think about it, he was limping before that. He could have faked falling so that if we noticed a limp or a scrape, we'd think that was where it came from."

"Why would he do that?"

"I bet he hurt himself climbing over a fence. Remember how smashed up the fences were? I don't think he can see very well in that costume and he must have hurt himself one night. He's pretty clumsy, after all, and the costume would be huge on him."

"Smart," Xena acknowledged. "The trick would have fooled us if you didn't have that photographic memory. Are you sure he was limping before?"

"Positive. And—"

Xena nudged him. "Hush! Look over there!"

As Xena and Xander strained their eyes they saw something large moving. It was the door of the stable, and it swung open slowly. It made a tiny creak and instantly stopped. After a pause it moved even more cautiously than before. The vague form outside the door disappeared inside the stable.

They waited in the silent darkness, so tense they could hardly breathe.

"The dogs didn't bark," Xander whispered into Xena's ear.

"I noticed," she whispered back. "They'd make some noise if someone they didn't know came in."

Still nothing. They didn't dare move. Xander's own heartbeat sounded like a drumbeat in his ears. Couldn't whoever was in there hear him?

"What's taking so long?" Xander whispered. Xena spread out her hands in an "I don't know" gesture. "Let's go look," Xander said.

They placed each foot carefully, freezing if there was even the least crackle. After what seemed like an hour they were at the door of the stable. Xena put her ear to the crack in the door, her head turned toward Xander.

That was when he saw it, a huge silent shape that loomed over his sister, massive arms upraised.

"Xena!" he cried. "Watch out!"

The creature took a step in Xander's direction. Xander flinched and stepped backward, tripping over something invisible in the moonlight and falling onto his back. He lay paralyzed, looking up at the Beast.

The creature gave a muffled roar. It wasn't the fearsome howling they'd heard before but sounded like a person trying to sound scary. This gave Xena courage, and the sight of the thing leaning over her little brother made her furious.

"Hold it right there!" she shouted, and the Beast, without looking around, leaped forward and took off running.

It never had a chance. It had no head start this time, and Xena's rage at the threat to Xander made her forget her twisted ankle. Almost immediately she reached the Beast and tackled it. She sat down hard on its back.

"*Oof!*" said the Beast. "Get off me!"

"No way," Xander said, joining Xena.

"Honest, I can't breathe. Get off me. I won't go anywhere."

Xena and Xander slid off the Beast's back, but they stayed near enough to stop any attempts to escape. It sat up and fumbled with something at its neck, then pulled off its shaggy head, revealing a familiar face peering up from the chest.

"Ian," Xander said. "I knew it!"

Chapter 21

Okay. You got me." Ian stood up. "Can you undo this? It takes me forever. Reaching around to the back is hard." Xena unsnapped him and Ian stepped out of the costume. "Sorry if I scared you."

"Sorry?" Xander asked. "Wasn't that what you were trying to do—scare people?"

"Well—yes," Ian admitted.

"Why?" Xena asked.

Instead of answering, Ian looked back at the house. Then he sighed and said, "I love this place, you know. I love everything about it."

"You sure don't act like it," Xander said. "Remember that first day we met you and you said it was dull here?"

"I know. I was just trying to convince myself I'd rather live in London. It made me sad to think that I'd never live here again. My parents were going to sell the paintings of my ancestors, and my great-grandfather's souvenirs from when he was an explorer, and—" He stopped, his voice a little shaky.

"What made you think of using the Beast costume to scare people?" Xena tried to change the subject.

When Ian answered, his voice was steadier. "Oh, I've always been crazy about the movies, and when the film students came and my parents gave them permission to use the property to film a documentary, I hung around and watched them a lot. I saw the Beast costume. I couldn't figure out how it fit into a documentary, but I didn't care. That Beast costume was really scary, especially in the dark, and it gave me an idea for how to stop the sale of the house. I even took some really old newspapers from the library to find out how the Beast acted when it was here before. I tried to return them but every time I go in, the librarian's watching, so I haven't been able to put them back."

Ian dug the toe of his shoe into the ground, and when he spoke again he sounded miserable. "I thought that if we didn't sell the house, my parents would come up with some other way to make money."

"Like what?" Xena asked.

"I don't know. Open a tearoom or give tours or something. But it's no good." Nobody spoke for a moment.

"Well," Xena said finally, "if you give me the newspapers, I can sneak them in without the librarian noticing." Ian looked as if he didn't believe her.

"Really, she can do it," Xander assured him. "People don't see her if she doesn't want them to."

"Okay." Ian picked up the Beast costume and disappeared into the stable with it, and then emerged again with a stack of yellowing newspapers in his arms. "Thanks," he said. "That librarian scares me."

"More than the Beast?" Xena asked, trying to make him laugh.

He didn't laugh, but his voice sounded more relaxed. "It's too late for you to cycle back to town. Why don't you spend the night? We have plenty of space."

"Cool!" Xander said. "I can't wait to see inside the house."

The house lived up to their wildest dreams. The rooms were huge, and there were fascinating things in most of them. A room like a den was decorated with exotic rugs and statues that Ian said had come from India, and in one of the sitting rooms (there were three) was the most enormous fireplace Xena and Xander had ever seen. It was topped by a mantel carved with strange twisted figures. Everywhere big paintings of ladies and gentlemen and fat babies hung on the walls.

Finally, after they had explored enough to satisfy even Xander, Ian showed them their bedroom. It was paneled in warm, dark wood. The two beds were so high there were step stools next to them for climbing in, and mattresses so soft Xena thought she might never want to get up.

When they woke the next morning the sun was shining brightly.

"What time is it?" Xander asked.

Xena, who seemed to have an internal clock, said, "Past ten o'clock, I think. Let's go find Ian."

When they reached the bottom of the huge sweeping staircase, they heard voices from inside one of the sitting rooms. Xena cracked open the door and peered in. There were Ian's parents, whom they had seen in the tourist office; the film crew that had been working on the Beast project; a man with a gray beard; and Ian. Xena caught Ian's attention and beckoned to him.

"You'll never believe it!" He came up to them, his eyes shining with happiness. "The best thing has happened!"

"What?" Xena and Xander asked together.

Ian pulled them a bit away from the door. "Do you see that man?" he asked, pointing through the opening to the gray-bearded man, who was now in deep conversation with Ian's parents. "He's the head of the film school. He came down to Blackslope to see how the students were coming along. And he's best friends with a famous director, and he said that his friend has been looking for a house and a property just like this to use for his next movie. They're going to pay my parents enough money that we'll be able to stay here!"

Xena and Xander said in chorus, "Wow! Congratulations!"

"And I'm going to work with them on the weekends and after school." Ian looked embarrassed. "Kind of to pay them back for messing with their things." He smiled at them and then waved as he went back into the sitting room.

"Let's go," Xena said. "We don't want Mom and Dad to start worrying." She put the newspapers into one of the bike's saddlebags and they took off for town.

The clock in the church tower struck eleven as they passed it. When they got back to the B and B, they found that Mrs. Roberts had left a pile of scones on the table and a note saying there was some cocoa ready for "hotting up" on the stove in the kitchen. She added that their parents were taking a last drive through the country and would be back soon to pick them up to go home to London.

As they were eating their late breakfast Xander said, "You know, Xena, we didn't really solve the mystery."

"What are you talking about?" She was indignant. "Of course we did!"

He shook his head. "I didn't mean *our* Beast mystery. I meant Sherlock's Beast, the one in the cold-case file. Plus there's still that missing sheep."

Xena thought for a moment. "I haven't heard anyone else say anything about the missing sheep since that day in the library. It must have found its way home. But you're right about Sherlock's case."

Suddenly she was as disappointed as her brother. She spread bright red preserves on her scone and took a bite. When Xander didn't answer her she looked up. He was sitting with a blank look in his eyes, his mouth hanging open. "Hello? Earth to Xander!"

He shook his head like a dog shaking water off itself. "I just thought of something! Quick— where are those newspapers that Ian had?"

They carefully washed all the crumbs and jam off their hands before touching the fragile old newspapers.

"It was something in one of the illustrations," Xander said. "Whoever drew the pictures made them look almost as realistic as photographs."

Xena looked over his shoulder. Ladies with feathered hats and gentlemen carrying skinny canes and wearing tight suits strolled arm in arm down a busy street. "What a funny little dog that lady has. And look, you can even read the signs on the wall." There were posters advertising a haberdashery, whatever that was, a charity tea, and a traveling circus. "Look at that!" She marveled at the intricate detail. "An aerialist? I wonder what that is."

"A trapeze artist." Xena didn't question him; she knew he had memorized most of the dictionary. "And look." He pointed to the circus poster. "They had a dancing bear and jugglers."

"Must have been a great circus!" Xena said.

Xander wasn't listening. Instead he pulled

out another paper, this one dated a week later. "Same circus in the next town, but nothing about a bear."

"Let me see," Xena said. Sure enough, there was no mention of a bear on the poster of the circus a week later in a different town.

"Hmm," she said, sitting back and closing her eyes. "I wonder . . ."

Xander sat still.

"I think I've got it." Xena opened her eyes. "What if they called it a dancing bear because it had a hurt foot, like it was missing a toe, and it walked funny?"

"The four-toed footprint!"

"Exactly," Xena said. "And what if the bear escaped from the circus, and people who saw it reported it as some kind of beast? They were so scared they imagined the beast had horns. The circus people wouldn't have told them what really happened, because they'd get in trouble for not keeping track of a dangerous animal, so they just moved on without reporting it. Maybe they found the bear, or maybe it lived in the woods for a while and then died. That's why they didn't advertise a dancing bear when they got to the next town. They didn't have one anymore!"

"But what about Adeline the cook?"

"I bet she ran away from that awful husband of hers," Xena said. "We'll never know for sure, but I bet she joined the circus."

Xander stood up and went upstairs. He came down with the cold-case notebook of their great ancestor, Sherlock Holmes. He rummaged around in a drawer of an end table and pulled out a pen and a pad of sticky notes. He tore one off and then took the notebook from Xena. He flipped to the page at the end of the section on the Beast of Blackslope, attached the note to it, and with a flourish wrote the words:

CASE CLOSED.

QUESTIONS FOR THE AUTHOR

TRACY BARRETT

What did you want to be when you grew up?
A poet, which is odd, since poetry is just about the only kind of writing that I don't do now! Later, I wanted to be an archaeologist, but then I discovered that archaeologists do most of their work in a trench in a hot part of the world in the middle of the summer, and that job lost a lot of its appeal.

What was your worst subject in school?
Does P.E. count as a subject? Because if it does, that was it.

What was your best subject in school?
Math was easy and fun for me until my senior year in high school when suddenly it was as though someone switched off a light and I couldn't get it anymore. I always did well in foreign languages. I liked English a lot but it wasn't one of my best subjects.

What was your first job?
I volunteered in a local hospital. If you were to ask me about my *strangest* job, though, it would have to be working as a benthic ecologist. That was the technical name, but my job was really being a "worm picker." I was helping with an experiment where scientists were trying to find out the effect of water pollution on the tiny critters that live in the mud. I would look through a microscope at a little dish full of sand and other things and pick out nematodes (which look like worms) and other things with tweezers.

Where do you write your books?
In my home office. I also have a day job as a college professor, but I never write there, and I never bring college work home with me. I've trained myself so well to write only at home and do my day-job work only at the office that the few times I've tried to write at the university, I haven't been able to!

Where do you find inspiration for your writing?
Inspiration is all around. It's sometimes hard to turn it off! Writers and non-writers all hear the same jokes, overhear the same strange conversations in the supermarket, read the same news stories, but the one who says, "Hmm, that would make a good story!" is the writer.

Which of your characters is most like you?
None of them are like me—at least I don't think so—but I based Ariadne in *Cold in Summer* on my daughter. In my next book, *King of Ithaka*, the main characters,

Telemachos and Brax, are exactly like my son, Patrick, and his best friend, Riley, but I didn't know I had based my characters on them until my husband pointed it out!

When you finish a book, who reads it first?
My daughter, and she's a good and tough critic. She finds all sorts of problems that never occurred to me.

Are you a morning person or a night owl?
I was a night owl for years and years, but gradually I've turned into more of a morning person. I do my most productive work in the morning and save the afternoon for things where I don't have to be creative.

What's your idea of the best meal ever?
Anything Italian, with something chocolate for dessert.

Which do you like better: cats or dogs?
Dogs, but only slightly. I love both!

What are you most afraid of?
Heights, which is why it's odd that I used to skydive. I met my husband when he helped me pack my parachute!

What time of year do you like best?
Tennessee, where I live, has a beautiful spring that lasts and lasts. When one kind of flower is starting to die out, another kind blooms. I love when the days get longer and we can sit on the porch after dinner and talk to our friends who walk by.

SQUARE FISH

If you could travel in time, where would you go?
I would love to see a dinosaur (if I knew it couldn't get to me), but most of the times in history that I'd most like to see involve interesting people. I'm fascinated by the Middle Ages and would love to see how people lived then, if I could be sure that I could get home to modern medicine and hot water and refrigeration.

What's the best advice you have ever received about writing?
Enjoy the process of writing because you never know if anyone else will ever read it. If you don't enjoy it, you might as well do something else.

What do you want readers to remember about your books?
I hope they remember the characters the most.

What would you do if you ever stopped writing?
I'd keep imagining stories. I would scratch them out in the sand if I were stuck on a desert island without paper and I would tell them to passing camels if I were stuck in the middle of the Sahara. What would I do for a job? I'd keep teaching Italian!

What do you consider to be your greatest accomplishment?
Raising two happy and nice kids to be happy and nice adults.

SQUARE FISH

For one day every one hundred years, the long-lost amulet of
the Egyptian god Thoth has the power to turn back time.

THAT DAY IS A WEEK FROM TODAY.

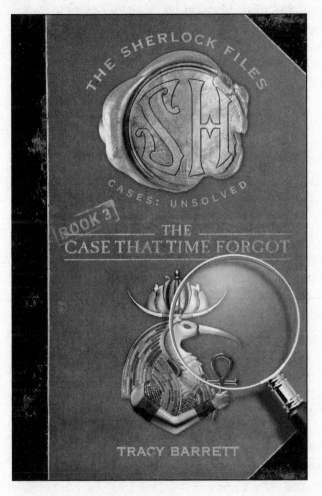

Will Xena and Xander be able to solve another
of Sherlock's unfinished cases? Find out in

——— THE ———
CASE THAT TIME FORGOT

Karim didn't have to tell Xander where to meet him. They both had after-school soccer practice—by now Xander was used to the way it was called "football" in England—and since they'd be practicing together, Xander was sure they'd have lots of chances to talk.

But it didn't turn out that way. It was a chilly, gray day, and the coach made them run laps to warm up. Karim was one of the fastest runners on the team, and every time he slowed down to keep pace with Xander, the coach shrilled on his whistle and yelled at him.

The two boys finally managed to meet in the locker room after practice.

"So what's up?" Xander asked as he changed out of his gym clothes. "What did you mean about a case that Sherlock Holmes worked on?"

"Shh!" Karim looked around. "Not so loud! You don't know who might be listening."

Xander looked around too. "Who?"

"I don't know. But I don't want anyone to know about this. It's—it's something that other people might be interested in. Let's wait until everyone's gone."

Lockers banged, boys talked and laughed, and after what seemed like a long time, they were alone.

Or almost. The janitor, Mr. Franklin, was mopping the floor, muttering about the dirt that the boys had tracked in. "Like there's anything we can do about that," Xander grumbled. "Cleats collect an awful lot of mud." Finally Mr. Franklin and his mop and bucket moved out into the hall.

"Okay," Xander said, "but you have to be quick. They're going to lock up the school any time now."

Karim launched right into his story. "Did you ever hear of the Carberry Museum?" Xander shook his head. "It's a really small place. Some guy named Josiah S. Carberry in the eighteen hundreds had this collection of stuff, mostly fossils and bones but some art too, ancient Greek and Mesopotamian and some Egyptian things."

"Sounds cool."

"It is. Anyway, after he died his house got turned into a museum. Mr. Carberry left a lot of money, and in his will he said that the trustees, the people who run the museum, should use it to buy things that they thought he'd like."

"What are you boys still doing here?"

Xander and Karim jumped and turned around. Mr. Singh, the assistant principal, had poked his head around the open door. "Football practice," they chorused.

"This late? Well, hurry up. I have some work to do in the office, but I want to leave soon."

"Yes, sir," Karim said, and the door closed.

"So about a hundred years ago," Karim went on, "the trustees bought an Egyptian water clock. Do you know what that is?"

It had been a while since Xander had studied ancient civilization back at home, but like many people, he was fascinated with ancient Egypt. He also had the help of his photographic memory and had read most of the encyclopedia. An image popped into his head.

"It's like a big jar, right?" Karim nodded. Xander continued, "And there's a hole at the bottom and lines marked on the inside, and the Egyptians filled it with water, and as it dripped out, they could tell what time it was by the level the water reached."

"Right. There are different kinds, but that's

like the one the trustees bought. It was carved from solid rock and weighed over a ton."

Xander whistled.

"I know. It was huge. So anyway, the Egyptian government sent it here with some other things, and it arrived at a warehouse to get unpacked and cleaned, and then they were going to take it to the Carberry Museum."

"They *were* going to take it to the museum? It never got there?"

"It vanished. Overnight. Everything else the Egyptians sent was still there, but some things got messed up. A mummy had been moved, and a part of it was broken—like someone maybe was looking for something under it—but the mummy was still there. Even a gold necklace wasn't missing. Just the water clock."

"So they called in Sherlock Holmes?" Of course they would ask for help from the most famous detective of the day, and that was his ancestor! Now that he thought of it, Xander remembered seeing a drawing of something that looked like a large flowerpot in the notebook of unsolved cases that he and Xena had been given by the SPFD. That must be the water clock!

Karim sat up straighter and looked sharply to his right. "What's that?"

"What?"

"Didn't you hear something?"

Xander strained his ears. "Nope. Nothing. Don't be paranoid. Everybody's gone except Mr. Singh."

"And Mr. Franklin."

"Nah. He finished here. Hurry up—before Mr. Singh comes back."

Karim walked over to the right-hand side of the locker room, glanced toward the showers, then returned. "Nothing there. Okay." But he still seemed nervous.

"Come *on*." Xander was dying of curiosity. "What else? Why do you care about a stolen water clock? How do you even know about it?"

Karim swallowed. He appeared strangely reluctant to go on. "There were guards watching over the clock." His voice dropped even lower. "And one of them—one of the guards was my great-great-great-granduncle. And—and he confessed that he stole it."

No wonder Karim was embarrassed to talk about the theft. Xander felt sorry for him, but he was more curious than ever. If Karim's ancestor had confessed to the crime, the case was solved. So why was the theft of the clock mentioned in the notebook of Holmes's *unsolved* cases? What kind of help did Karim want? And why did he come to Xena and Xander right now? Why not months ago, when everyone first found out that they were related to the great detective who had lived a hundred years earlier?

Before Xander could ask, a few musical notes sounded from Karim's backpack. He pulled out his cell phone. "Hi, Mom. Practice ran late." He glanced anxiously at Xander. "I'm still in the locker room. No, I'm fine. Okay, five minutes. Bye." He snapped the phone shut. "I have to be quick. The water clock wasn't the only thing stolen."

"But I thought you said—"

Karim held up his hand. "Please, Xander, let me finish. I went to see my grandparents over the weekend. My granddad is ill." He gulped. "He—he was worried he was going to die, even though my dad says he'll be fine. My granddad said he had something to tell me that should be handed down from father to son. He told my father, but my father didn't believe him, so he had to tell me."

Xander felt a prickle of excitement. "What was it?"

"He told me about the water clock. He said it had a secret compartment, and inside it was a magic amulet that no one's ever found."

Xander's mind was whirring. "An amulet—you mean like a charm?" Karim nodded. "And it's *magic*?"

"That's what my granddad said." Karim lowered his voice even further and said, "Every fifty years, the amulet can make time stand still. And on Saturday"— he was practically whispering by now—"the fifty years will be up. The amulet's magic will work!"

THINK YOU'RE A SUPER-SLEUTH?
HAVE WE GOT A MYSTERY FOR YOU...

The 100-Year-Old Secret
Tracy Barrett
978-0-312-60212-3
$6.99 US / $8.50 Can

Masterpiece
Elise Broach
978-0-312-60870-5
$7.99 US / $9.99 Can

Shakespeare's Secret
Elise Broach
978-0-312-37132-6
$5.99 US / $6.99 Can

Steinbeck's Ghost
Lewis Buzbee
978-0-312-60211-6
$7.99 US / $9.99 Can

The Ghost of Fossil Glen
Cynthia DeFelice
978-0-312-60213-0
$6.99 US / $8.50 Can

The Diamond of Drury Lane
Julia Golding
978-0-312-56123-9
$7.99 US

The Trolls
Polly Horvath
978-0-312-38419-7
$6.99 US / $7.99 Can

The Young Unicorns
Madeleine L'Engle
978-0-312-37933-9
$7.99 US / $8.99 Can

Danger in the Dark
Tom Lalicki
978-0-312-60214-7
$6.99 US / $8.50 Can

SQUARE FISH
WWW.SQUAREFISHBOOKS.COM
AVAILABLE WHEREVER BOOKS ARE SOLD